Seawitch

SEAWITCH

Alistair MacLean

BOOK CLUB ASSOCIATES
LONDON

This edition published 1977 by
Book Club Associates

By arrangement with Wm. Collins Sons & Co. Ltd.

First published 1977
© Alistair MacLean 1977
Set in Monotype Baskerville
Made and Printed in Great Britain by
William Collins Sons & Co. Ltd, Glasgow

To Lachan

prologue

Normally there are only two types of marine machines concerned with the discovery and recovery of oil from under the ocean floor. The first one, which is mainly engaged in the discovery of oil, is a self-propelled vessel, sometimes of very considerable size. Apart from its towering drilling derrick, it is indistinguishable from any ocean-going cargo vessel; its purpose is to drill bore-holes in areas where seismological and geological studies suggest oil may exist. The technical operation of this activity is highly complex, yet these vessels have achieved a remarkable level of success. However, they suffer from two major drawbacks. Although they are equipped with the most advanced and sophisticated navigational equipment, including bow-thrust propellers, for them to maintain position in running seas, strong tides and winds when boring can be extremely difficult; and in really heavy weather operations have to be suspended.

For the actual drilling of oil and its recovery – principally its recovery – the so-called 'jack-up system' is in almost universal use. A rig of this type has to be towed into position, and consists of a platform which carries the drilling rig, cranes, helipads and all essential services, including living accommodation, and is attached to the seabed by firmly anchored legs. In normal conditions it is extremely effective, but like the discovery ships it has drawbacks. It is not mobile. It has to suspend operations in even moderately heavy weather. And it can be used only in comparatively shallow water: the deepest is in the North Sea, where most of those rigs are to be found.

This North Sea rig stands in about four hundred and fifty feet of water and the cost of increasing the length of those legs would be so prohibitive as to make oil recovery quite uneconomical, even although there are plans for the Americans to construct a rig with eight-hundred-feet legs off the Californian coast. There is also the unknown safety factor. Two such rigs have already been lost in the North Sea. The cause of those disasters has not been clearly evaluated, although it is suspected, obviously not without cause, that there may have been design, structural or metallic faults in one or more of the legs.

And then there is the third type of oil rig – the TLP – technically, the tension leg drilling/production platform. At the time of this story there was only one of its type in the world. The platform – the working area – was about the size of a football field – if, that is, one can imagine a triangular football field, for the platform was, in fact, an equilateral triangle. The deck was not made of steel but of a uniquely designed ferro-concrete, specially developed by a Dutch oil ship-building company. The supports for this massive platform had been designed and built in England and consisted of three enormous steel legs, each at one corner of the structure, all three being joined together by a variety of horizontal and diagonal hollow cylinders, the total combination offering so tremendous a degree of buoyancy that the working platform they supported was out of the reach of even the highest waves.

From each of the bases of the three legs, three massive steel cables extended to the base of the ocean floor, where each triple set was attached to large sea-floor anchors. Powerful motors could raise or lower those cables at will so that those anchors could be lowered to a depth two or three times that of most modern fixed oil derricks, which meant that it could operate at depths far out on the continental shelf.

8

The TLP had other very considerable advantages.

Its great buoyancy put the anchor cables under constant tension, and this tension practically eliminated the heaving, pitching and rolling of the platform. Thus the rig could continue operating in very severe storms, storms that would automatically stop production on any other type of derrick.

It was also virtually immune to the effects of an under-sea earthquake.

It was also mobile. It had only to up anchors to move to potentially more productive areas.

And compared to standard oil rigs its cost of establishing position in any given spot was so negligible as to be worth no more than a passing mention.

The name of the TLP was the *Seawitch*.

chapter

1

In certain places and among certain people, the *Seawitch* was a very bad name indeed. But, overwhelmingly, their venom was reserved for a certain Lord Worth, a multi – some said bulti – millionaire, chairman and sole owner of Worth Hudson Oil Company and, incidentally, owner of the *Seawitch*. When his name was mentioned by any of the ten men present at that shoreside house on Lake Tahoe, it was in tones of less than hushed reverence.

Their meeting was announced in neither the national nor local press. This was due to two factors. The delegates arrived and departed either singly or in couples and among the heterogeneous summer population of Lake Tahoe such comings and goings went unremarked or were ignored. More importantly, the delegates to the meeting were understandably reluctant that their assembly become common knowledge. The day was Friday 13th, a date that boded no good for someone.

There were nine delegates present, plus their host. Four of them were American, but only two of these mattered – Corral, who represented the oil and mineral leases in the Florida area, and Benson, who represented the rigs off Southern California.

Of the other six, again only two mattered. One was Patinos of Venezuela; the other was Borosoff of Russia: his interest in American oil supplies could only be regarded as minimal. It was widely assumed amongst the others that his main interest in attending the meeting was to stir up as much trouble as possible, an assumption that was probably correct.

All ten were, in various degrees, suppliers of oil to the United States and had the one common interest: to see that the price of those supplies did not drop. The last thing they all wanted to see was an oil value depreciation.

Benson, whose holiday home this was and who was nominally hosting the meeting, opened the discussion.

'Gentlemen, does anyone have any strong objections if I bring a third party – that is, a man who represents neither ourselves nor Lord Worth – into this meeting?'

Practically everyone had, and there were some moments of bedlamic confusion: they had not only objections but very strong ones at that.

Borosoff, the Russian, said: 'No. It is too dangerous.' He glanced around the group with calculated suspiciousness. 'There are already too many of us privy to these discussions '

Benson, who had not become head of one of Europe's biggest oil companies, a British-based one, just because someone had handed him the job as a birthday present, could be disconcertingly blunt.

'You, Borosoff, are the one with the slenderest claims to be present at this meeting. You might well bear that in mind. Name your suspect.' Borosoff remained silent. 'Bear in mind, gentlemen, the objective of this meeting – to maintain, at least, the present oil price levels. The OPEC is now actively considering hiking all oil prices That doesn't hurt us much here in the US - we'll just hike our own prices and pass them on to the public '

Patinos said: 'You're every bit as unscrupulous and ruthless as you claim us to be.'

'Realism is not the same as ruthlessness. Nobody's going to hike anything while Worth Hudson is around

They are already undercutting us, the majors A slight pinch, but we feel it. If we raise our prices more and their's remain steady, the slight pinch is going to increase. And if they get some more TLPs into operation then the pinch will be beginning to hurt. It will also hurt the OPEC, for the demand for your products will undoubtedly fall off.

'We all subscribe to the gentlemen's agreement among major oil companies that they will not prospect for oil in international waters, that is to say outside their own legally and internationally recognized territorial limits. Without observance of this agreement, the possibilities of legal, diplomatic, political and international strife, ranging from scenes of political violence to outright armed confrontation, are only too real. Let us suppose that Nation A – as some countries have already done – claims all rights for all waters a hundred miles offshore from its coasts. Let us further suppose that Nation B comes along and starts drilling thirty miles outside those limits. Then, horror of horrors, let us suppose that Nation A makes a unilateral decision to extend its offshore limits to a hundred and fifty miles – and don't forget that Peru has claimed two hundred miles as its limits: the subsequent possibilities are too awesome to contemplate.

'Alas, not all are gentlemen. The chairman of the Worth Hudson Oil Company, Lord Worth, and his entire pestiferous board of directors, would have been the first vehemently to deny any suggestion that they were gentlemen, a fact held in almost universal acceptance by their competitors in oil. They would also equally vehemently have denied that they were criminals, a fact that may or may not have been true, but most certainly is not true now.

'He has, in short, committed what should be two indictable offences. "Should," I say. The first is unprovable, the second, although an offence in moral terms, is not, as yet, strictly illegal.

'The facts of the first – and what I consider much the minor offence – concerns the building of Lord Worth's TLP in Houston. It is no secret in the industry that the plans for those were stolen – those for the platform from the Mobil Oil Company, those for the legs and anchoring systems from the Chevron Oilfield Research Company. But, as I say, unprovable. It is commonplace for new inventions and developments to occur at two or more places simultaneously, and he can always claim that his design team, working in secret, beat the others to the gun.'

In saying which Benson was perfectly correct. In the design of the *Seawitch* Lord Worth had adopted short-cuts which the narrow-minded could have regarded as unscrupulous if not illegal. Like all oil companies, Worth Hudson had its own design team. As they were all cronies of Lord Worth and were employed for purely tax-deductible purposes, their combined talents would have been incapable of designing a rowing boat.

This didn't worry Lord Worth. He didn't need a design team. He was a vastly wealthy man, had powerful friends – none of them, needless to say, among the oil companies – and was a master of industrial espionage. With the resources at his disposal he found little trouble in obtaining those two secret advance plans, which he passed on to a firm of highly competent marine designers, whose exorbitant fees were matched only by their extreme discretion. The designers found little difficulty in marrying the two sets of plans, adding just sufficient modifications and improvements to discourage those with a penchant for patent rights litigation.

Benson went on: 'But what really worries me, and what should worry all you gentlemen here, is Lord Worth's violation of the tacit agreement never to indulge ın drilling in international waters.' He paused, deliberately for effect, and looked slowly at each of the other nine in turn. 'I say in all seriousness, gentlemen, that Lord Worth's foolhardiness and greed may well prove to be the spark that triggers off the ignition of a third world war. Apart from protecting our own interests I maintain that for the good of mankind – and I speak from no motive of spurious self-justification – if the governments of the world do not intervene then the imperative is that we should. As the governments show no signs of intervention, then I suggest that the burden lies upon us. This madman must be stopped. I think you gentlemen would agree that only we realize the full implications of all of this and that only we have the technical expertise to stop him.'

There were murmurs of approval from around the room. A sincere and disinterested concern for the good of mankind was a much more morally justifiable reason for action than the protection of one's own selfish interests. Patinos, the man from Venezuela, looked at Benson with a smile of mild cynicism on his face. The smile signified nothing. Patinos, a sincere and devout Catholic, wore the same expression when he passed through the doors of his church.

'You seem very sure of this, Mr Benson?'

'I've given quite some thought to it.'

Borosoff said: 'And quite how do you propose to stop this madman, Mr Benson?'

'I don't know.'

'You don't know?' One of the others at the table lifted his eyebrows about a millimetre – which, for him, was a sign of complete disapproval. 'Then why did you summon us all this distance?'

'I didn't summon you. I asked you. I asked you to approve whatever course of action we might take.'

'This course of action being? –

'Again, I don't know.'

The eyebrows returned to normal. A twitch of the man's lip showed that he was contemplating smiling.

'This – ah – third party?'

'Yes.'

'He has a name?'

'Cronkite. John Cronkite.'

A hush descended upon the company. The open objections had turned into pensive hesitation which in turn gave way to a nodding acceptance. Benson apart, no one there had ever met Cronkite, but his name was a household word to all of them. In the oil business his name had in his own lifetime long become a legend, although at times a far from savoury one. They all knew that any of them might require his incomparable services at any time, while at the same time hoping that that day would never come.

When it came to the capping of blazing gushers, Cronkite was without peer. Wherever in the world a gusher blew fire no one even considered putting it out themselves, they just sent for Cronkite. To wincing observers his *modus operandi* seemed nothing short of Draconian, but Cronkite would blasphemously brook no interference. Despite the extortionate fees he charged it was more common than not for a four-engined jet to be put at his disposal to get him to the scene of the disaster as quickly as possible. Cronkite always delivered. He also knew all there was to know about the oil business. And he was, hardly surprisingly, extremely tough and utterly ruthless.

Henderson, who represented oil interests in Honduras, said: 'Why should a man with his extraordinary quali-fications, the world's number one, as we all know, choose to engage himself in – ah – an enterprise of this nature? From his reputation I would hardly have thought that he was one to be concerned about the woes of suffering mankind.'

'He isn't. Money. Cronkite comes very high. A fresh challenge – the man's a born adventurer. But, basically, it's because he hates Lord Worth's guts.'

Henderson said: 'Not an uncommon sentiment, it seems. Why?'

'Lord Worth sent his own private Boeing for him to come cap a blazing gusher in the Middle East. By the time Cronkite arrived Lord Worth's own men had capped it. This, alone, Cronkite regarded as a mortal insult. He then made the mistake of demanding the full fee for his services Lord Worth has a reputation for notorious Scottish meanness, which, while an insult to the Scots, is more than justified in his case. He refused, and said that he would pay him for his time, no more. Cronkite then compounded his error by taking him to court. With the kind of lawyers Lord Worth can afford, Cronkite never had a chance. Not only did he lose but he had to pay the costs.'

'Which wouldn't be low?' Henderson said.

'Medium-high to massive. I don't know. All I know is that Cronkite has done quite a bit of brooding about it ever since.'

'Such a man would not have to be sworn to secrecy?'

'A man can swear a hundred different oaths and break them all. Besides, because of the exorbitant fees Cronkite charges, his feeling towards Lord Worth and the fact that he might just have to step outside the law, his silence is ensured.'

It was the turn of another of those grouped round the table to raise his eyebrows. 'Outside the law? We cannot risk being involved – '

' "Might," I said. For us, the element of risk does not exist '

'May we see this man?'

Benson nodded, rose, went to a door and admitted Cronkite.

Cronkite was a Texan. In height, build and cragginess of features he bore a remarkable resemblance to John Wayne. Unlike Wayne he never smiled. His face was of a peculiarly yellow complexion, typical of those who have had an overdose of anti-malarial tablets, which was just what had happened to Cronkite. Mepacrine does not make for a peaches and cream complexion – not that Cronkite had ever had anything even remotely resembling that. He was newly returned from Indonesia, where he had inevitably maintained his hundred per cent record.

'Mr Cronkite,' Benson said. 'Mr Cronkite, this is – '

Cronkite was brusque. In a gravelly voice he said: 'I do not wish to know their names.'

In spite of the abruptness of his tone, several of the oilmen round the table almost beamed. Here was a man of discretion, a man after their own hearts.

Cronkite went on: 'All I understand from Mr Benson is that I am required to attend to a matter involving Lord Worth and the *Seawitch*. Mr Benson has given me a pretty full briefing. I know the background. I would like, first of all, to hear any suggestions you gentlemen may have to offer.' Cronkite sat down, lit what proved to be a very foul-smelling cigar, and waited expectantly

He kept silent during the following half-hour discussion For ten of the world's top businessmen they proved to be an extraordinarily inept, not to say inane lot. They talked in an ever-narrowing series of concentric circles.

Henderson said: 'First of all it must be agreed that there is no violence to be used. Is it so agreed?'

Everybody nodded their agreement. Each and every one of them was a pillar of business respectability who could not afford to have his reputation besmirched in anv way. No one appeared to notice that Cronkite sat motion-less as a graven image. Except for lifting a hand to puff out increasingly vile clouds of smoke, Cronkite did not move throughout the discussion. He also remained totally silent.

After agreeing that there should be no violence the meeting of ten agreed on nothing.

Finally Patinos spoke up. 'Why don't you – one of you four Americans, I mean – approach your Congress to pass an emergency law banning off-shore drilling in extra-territorial waters?'

Benson looked at him with something akin to pity. 'I am afraid, sir, that you do not quite understand the relations between the American majors and Congress. On the few occasions we have met with them – something to do with too much profits and too little tax – I'm afraid we have treated them in so – ah – cavalier a fashion that nothing would give them greater pleasure than to refuse any request we might make.'

One of the others, known simply as 'Mr A', said: 'How about an approach to that international legal ombudsman, the Hague? After all, this is an international matter.'

'Not on.' Henderson shook his head. 'Forget it. The dilatoriness of that august body is so legendary that all present would be long retired – or worse – before a decision is made. The decision would just as likely be negative anyway.'

'UNO?' Mr A said.

'That talk-shop!' Benson had obviously a low and not uncommon view of the UNO. 'They haven't even the power to order New York to install a new parking meter outside their front door.'

The next revolutionary idea came from one of the Americans.

'Why shouldn't we all agree, for an unspecified time –

let's see how it goes – to *lower* our price below that of Worth Hudson. In that case no one would want to buy their oil.'

This proposal was met with a stunned disbelief.

Corral spoke in a kind voice. 'Not only would that lead to vast losses to the major oil companies, but would almost certainly and immediately lead Lord Worth to lower *his* prices fractionally below their new ones. The man has sufficient working capital to keep him going for a hundred years at a loss – in the unlikely event, that is, of his running at a loss at all.'

A lengthy silence followed. Cronkite was not quite as immobile as he had been. The granitic expression on his face remained unchanged but the fingers of his non-smoking hand had begun to drum gently on the arm-rest of his chair. For Cronkite, this was equivalent to throwing a fit of hysterics.

It was during this period that all thoughts of the ten of maintaining their high, gentlemanly and ethical standards against drilling in international waters was forgotten.

'Why not,' Mr A said, 'buy him out?' In fairness to Mr A it has to be said that he did not appreciate just how wealthy Lord Worth was and that, immensely wealthy though he, Mr A, was, Lord Worth could have bought him out lock, stock and barrel. 'The *Seawitch* rights, I mean. A hundred million dollars. Let's be generous, two hundred million dollars. Why not?'

Corral looked depressed. 'The answer "why not" is easy. By the latest reckoning Lord Worth is one of the world's five richest men and even two hundred million dollars would only come into the category of pennies as far as he was concerned.'

Mr A looked depressed.

Benson said: 'Sure, he'd sell.'

Mr A visibly brightened

'For two reasons only. In the first place he'd make a quick and splendid profit. In the second place, for less than half the selling price, he could build another *Seawitch*, anchor it a couple of miles away from the present *Seawitch* – there are no leasehold rights in extra-territorial waters – and start sending oil ashore at his same old price.'

A temporarily deflated Mr A slumped back in his armchair.

'A partnership, then,' Mr A said. His tone was that of a man in a state of quiet despair.

'Out of the question.' Henderson was very positive. 'Like all very rich men, Lord Worth is a born loner. He wouldn't have a combined partnership with the King of Saudi Arabia and the Shah of Persia even if it had been offered him.'

In a pall-like gloom a baffled and exhausted silence fell upon the embattled ten. A thoroughly bored and hitherto wordless John Cronkite rose.

He said without preamble: 'My personal fee will be one million dollars. I will require ten million dollars for operating expenses. Every cent of this will be accounted for and the unspent balance returned. I demand a completely free hand and no interference from any of you. If I do encounter any such interference I shall retain the balance of the expenses and at the same time abandon the mission. I refuse to disclose what my plans are – or will be when I have formulated them. Finally, I would prefer to have no further contact with any of you, now or at any time.'

The certainty and confidence of the man were astonishing. Agreement among the mightily-relieved ten was immediate and total. The ten million dollars – a trifling sum to those accustomed to spending as much in bribes every month or so – would be delivered within twenty-four, at the most forty-eight hours to a Cuban numbered account in Miami – the only place in the United States where Swiss-type numbered accounts were permitted. For tax evasion purposes the money, of course, would not come from any of their respective countries: instead, ironically enough, from their bulging off-shore funds.

chapter
2

Lord Worth was tall, lean and erect. His complexion was of the mahogany hue of the playboy millionaire who spends his life in the sun: Lord Worth seldom worked less than sixteen hours a day. His abundant hair and moustache were snow-white. According to his mood and expression and to the eye of the beholder he could have been a Biblical patriarch, a better-class Roman senator or a gentlemanly seventeenth-century pirate - except for the fact, of course, that none of those ever, far less habitually, wore lightweight alpaca suits of the same colour as Lord Worth's hair.

He looked and was every inch an aristocrat. Unlike the many Americans who bore the Christian names of Duke or Earl, Lord Worth really was a lord, the fifteenth in succession of a highly distinguished family of Scottish peers of the realm. The fact that their distinction had lain mainly in the fields of assassination, endless clan warfare, the stealing of women and cattle and the selling of their fellow peers down the river was beside the point: the earlier Scottish peers didn't go in too much for the more cultural activities. The blue blood that had run in their veins ran in Lord Worth's. As ruthless, predatory, acquisitive and courageous as any of his ancestors, Lord Worth simply went about his business with a degree of refinement and sophistication that would have lain several light years beyond their understanding.

He had reversed the trend of Canadians coming to Britain, making their fortunes and eventually being elevated to the peerage: he had already been a peer, and an extremely wealthy one, before emigrating to Canada. His emigration, which had been discreet and precipitous, had not been entirely voluntary. He had made a fortune in real estate in London before the Internal Revenue had become embarrassingly interested in his activities. Fortunately for him, whatever charges which might have been laid against his door were not extraditable.

He had spent several years in Canada, investing his millions in the Worth Hudson Oil Company and proving himself to be even more able in the oil business than he had been in real estate. His tankers and refineries spanned the globe before he had decided that the climate was too cold for him and moved south to Florida. His splendid mansion was the envy of the many millionaires – of a lesser financial breed, admittedly – who almost literally jostled for elbow-room in the Fort Lauderdale area.

The dining-room in that mansion was something to behold. Monks, by the very nature of their calling, are supposed to be devoid of all earthly lusts, but no monk, past or present, could ever have gazed on the gleaming magnificence of that splendid oaken refectory table without turning pale chartreuse in envy. The chairs, inevitably, were Louis XIV. The splendidly embroidered silken carpet, with a pile deep enough for a fair-sized mouse to take cover in, would have been judged by an expert to come from Damascus and to have cost a fortune: the expert would have been right on both counts. The heavy drapes and embroidered silken walls were of the same pale grey, the latter being enhanced by a series of original Impressionist paintings, no less than three by Matisse and the same number by Renoir. Lord Worth was no dilettante and was clearly trying to make amends for his ancestors' shortcomings in the cultural fields.

It was in those suitably princely surroundings that Lord Worth was at the moment taking his ease, revelling in his second brandy and the company of the two beings whom – after money – he loved most in the world: his two daughters Marina and Melinda, who had been so named by their now divorced Spanish mother. Both were young, both were beautiful, and could have been mistaken for twins, which they weren't: they were easily distinguishable by the fact that while Marina's hair was black as a raven's wing Melinda's was pure titian.

There were two other guests at the table. Many a local millionaire would have given a fair slice of his ill-gotten gains for the privilege and honour of sitting at Lord Worth's table. Few were invited, and then but seldom. These two young men, comparatively as poor as church mice, had the unique privilege, without invitation, of coming and going as they pleased, which was pretty often.

Mitchell and Roomer were two pleasant men in their early thirties for whom Lord Worth had a strong if concealed admiration and whom he held in something close to awe – inasmuch as they were the only two completely honest men he had ever met. Not that Lord Worth had ever stepped on the wrong side of the law, although he frequently had a clear view of what happened on the other side: it was simply that he was not in the habit of dealing with honest men. They had both been highly efficient police sergeants, only they had been too efficient, much given to arresting the wrong people such as crooked politicians and equally crooked wealthy businessmen who had previously laboured under the mis-apprehension that they were above the law. They were fired, not to put too fine a point on it, for their total incorruptibility.

Of the two Michael Mitchell was the taller, the

broader and the less good-looking. With slightly craggy face, ruffled dark hair and blue chin, he could never have made it as a matinée idol. John Roomer, with his brown hair and trimmed brown moustache, was altogether better-looking. Both were shrewd, intelligent and highly experienced. Roomer was the intuitive one, Mitchell the one long on action. Apart from being charming both men were astute and highly resourceful. And they were possessed of one other not inconsiderable quality: both were deadly marksmen.

Two years previously they had set up their own private investigative practice, and in that brief space of time had established such a reputation that people in real trouble now made a practice of going to them instead of to the police, a fact that hardly endeared them to the local law. Their homes and combined office were within two miles of Lord Worth's estate where, as said, they were frequent and welcome visitors. That they did not come for the exclusive pleasure of his company Lord Worth was well aware. Nor, he knew, were they even in the slightest way interested in his money, a fact that Lord Worth found astonishing, as he had never previously encountered anyone who wasn't thus interested. What they were interested in, and deeply so, were Marina and Melinda.

The door opened and Lord Worth's butler, Jenkins English, of course, as were the two footmen – made his usual soundless entrance, approached the head of the table and murmured discreetly in Lord Worth's ear. Lord Worth nodded and rose.

'Excuse me, girls, gentlemen. Visitors. I'm sure you can get along together quite well without me.' He made his way to his study, entered and closed the door behind him, a very special padded door that, when shut, rendered the room completely soundproof.

The study, in its own way - Lord Worth was no sybarite

but he liked his creature comforts as well as the next man ·
was as sumptuous as the dining-room· oak, leather, a
wholly unnecessary log fire burning in one corner all
straight from the best English baronial mansions. The
walls were lined with thousands of books, many of which
Lord Worth had actually read, a fact that must have
caused great distress to his illiterate ancestors, who had
despised degeneracy above all else.

A tall bronzed man with aquiline features and grey
hair rose to his feet. Both men smiled and shook hands
warmly

Lord Worth said: 'Corral, my dear chap! How very
nice to see you again. It's been quite some time

'My pleasure, Lord Worth. Nothing recently that
would have interested you.'

'But now?'

'Now is something else again.'

The Corral who stood before Lord Worth was indeed
the Corral who, in his capacity as representative of the
Florida off-shore leases, had been present at the meeting
of ten at Lake Tahoe. Some years had passed since he and
Lord Worth had arrived at an amicable and mutually
satisfactory agreement. Corral, widely regarded as Lord
Worth's most avowedly determined enemy and certainly
the most vociferous of his critics, reported regularly to
Lord Worth on the current activities and, more importantly, the projected plans of the major companies,
which didn't hurt Lord Worth at all. Corral, in return,
received an annual tax-free retainer of $200,000, which
didn't hurt him very much either.

Lord Worth pressed a bell and within seconds Jenkins
entered bearing a silver tray with two large brandies.
There was no telepathy involved, just years of experience
and a long-established foreknowledge of Lord Worth's
desires. When he left both men sat

27

Lord Worth said: 'Well, what news from the west?'

'The Cherokee, I regret to say, are after you.'

Lord Worth sighed and said: 'It had to come some time. Tell me all.'

Corral told him all. He had a near-photographic memory and a gift for concise and accurate reportage. Within five minutes Lord Worth knew all that was worth knowing about the Lake Tahoe meeting.

Lord Worth who, because of the unfortunate mis-understanding that had arisen between himself and Cronkite, knew the latter as well as any and better than most, said at the end of Corral's report: 'Did Cronkite subscribe to the ten's agreement to abjure any form of violence?'

'No.'

'Not that it would have mattered if he had. Man's a total stranger to the truth. And ten million dollars expenses, you tell me?'

'It did seem a bit excessive '

'Can you see a massive outlay like that being con-comitant with anything except violence?'

'No.'

'Do you think the others believed that there was no connection between them?'

'Let me put it this way, sir. Any group of people who can convince themselves, or appear to convince them-selves, that any action proposed to be taken against you is for the betterment of mankind is also prepared to con-vince themselves, or appear to convince themselves, that the word "Cronkite" is synonymous with peace on earth.

'So their consciences are clear. If Cronkite goes to any excessive lengths in death and destruction to achieve their ends they can always throw up their hands in horror and say, "Good God, we never thought the man would go that far." Not that any connection between them and

Cronkite would ever be established. What a bunch of devious, mealy-mouthed hypocrites!'

He paused for a moment.

'I suppose Cronkite refused to divulge his plans?'

'Absolutely. But there is one little and odd circumstance that I've kept for the end. Just as we were leaving Cronkite drew two of the ten to one side and spoke to them privately. It would be interesting to know why.'

'Any chance of finding out?'

'A fair chance. Nothing guaranteed. But I'm sure Benson could find out – after all, it was Benson who invited us all to Lake Tahoe.'

'And you think you could persuade Benson to tell you?'

'A fair chance. Nothing more.'

Lord Worth put on his resigned expression. 'All right, how much?'

'Nothing. Money won't buy Benson.' Corral shook his head in disbelief. 'Extraordinary, in this day and age, but Benson is not a mercenary man. But he does owe me the odd favour, one of them being that, without me, he wouldn't be the president of the oil company that he is now.' Corral paused. 'I'm surprised you haven't asked me the identities of the two men Cronkite took aside.'

'So am I.'

'Borosoff of the Soviet Union and Patinos of Venezuela.' Lord Worth appeared to lapse into a trance. 'That mean anything to you?'

Lord Worth bestirred himself. 'Yes. Units of the Russian navy are making a so-called "goodwill tour" of the Caribbean. They are, inevitably, based on Cuba. Of the ten, those are the only two that could bring swift – ah - naval intervention to bear against the *Seawitch*.' He shook his head. 'Diabolical. Utterly diabolical.'

'My way of thinking too, sir. There's no knowing. But I'll check as soon as possible and hope to get results.'

'And I shall take immediate precautions.' Both men rose. 'Corral, we shall have to give serious consideration to the question of increasing this paltry retainer of yours.'

'We try to be of service, Lord Worth.'

Lord Worth's private radio room bore more than a passing resemblance to the flight deck of his private 707. The variety of knobs, switches, buttons and dials was bewildering. Lord Worth seemed perfectly at home with them all, and proceeded to make a number of calls.

The first of these were to his four helicopter pilots, instructing them to have his two largest helicopters – never a man to do things by halves, Lord Worth owned no fewer than six of these machines – ready at his own private airfield shortly before dawn. The next four were to people of whose existence his fellow directors were totally unaware. The first was to Cuba, the second to Venezuela. Lord Worth's world-wide range of contacts – employees, rather – was vast. The instructions to both were simple and explicit. A constant monitoring watch was to be kept on the naval bases in both countries, and any sudden and expected departures of any naval vessels, and their type, was to be reported to him immediately.

The third, to a person who lived not too many miles away, was addressed to a certain Giuseppe Palermo, whose name sounded as if he might be a member of the Mafia, but who definitely wasn't: the Mafia Palermo despised as a mollycoddling organization which had become so ludicrously gentle in its methods of persuasion as to be in imminent danger of becoming respectable. The next call was to Baton Rouge in Louisiana, where there lived a person who only called himself 'Conde' and whose main claim to fame lay in the fact that he was the highest-ranking naval officer to have been court-martialled and dishonourably discharged since World

War Two. He, like the others, received very explicit instructions. Not only was Lord Worth a master organizer, but the efficiency he displayed was matched only by his speed in operation.

The noble lord, who would have stoutly maintained – if anyone had the temerity to accuse him, which no one ever had – that he was no criminal, was about to become just that. Even this he would have strongly denied and that on three grounds. The Constitution upheld the rights of every citizen to bear arms; every man had the right to defend himself and his property against criminal attack by whatever means lay to hand; and the only way to fight fire was with fire.

The final call Lord Worth put through, and this time with total confidence, was to his tried and trusted lieutenant, Commander Larsen.

Commander Larsen was the captain of the *Seawitch*.

Larsen – no one knew why he called himself 'Commander', and he wasn't the kind of person you asked – was a rather different breed of man from his employer. Except in a public court or in the presence of a law officer he would cheerfully admit to anyone that he was both a non-gentleman *and* a criminal. And he certainly bore no resemblance to any aristocrat, alive or dead. But for all that there did exist a genuine rapport and mutual respect between Lord Worth and himself. In all likelihood they were simply brothers under the skin.

As a criminal and non-aristocrat – and casting no aspersions on honest unfortunates who may resemble him – he certainly looked the part. He had the general build and appearance of the more viciously daunting heavyweight wrestler, deep-set black eyes that peered out under the overhanging foliage of hugely bushy eyebrows, an equally bushy black beard, a hooked nose and a face that looked as if it had been in regular contact with a series of heavy objects. No one, with the possible exception of Lord Worth, knew who he was, what he had been or from where he had come. His voice, when he spoke, came as a positive shock: beneath that Neanderthaloid façade was the voice and the mind of an educated man. It really ought not to have come as such a shock: beneath the façade of many an exquisite fop lies the mind of a retarded fourth-grader.

Larsen was in the radio room at that moment, listening attentively, nodding from time to time, then flicked a switch that put the incoming call on to the loudspeaker.

He said: 'All clear, sir. Everything understood. We'll make the preparations. But haven't you overlooked something, sir?'

'Overlooked what?' Lord Worth's voice over the telephone carried the overtones of a man who couldn't possibly have overlooked anything.

'You've suggested that armed surface vessels may be used against us. If they're prepared to go to such lengths isn't it feasible that they'll go to any lengths?'

'Get to the point, man.'

'The point is that it's easy enough to keep an eye on a couple of naval bases. But I suggest it's a bit more difficult to keep an eye on a dozen, maybe two dozen airfields.'

'Good God!' There was a long pause during which the rattle of cogs and the meshing of gear-wheels in Lord Worth's brain couldn't be heard. 'Do you really think – '

'If I were on the *Seawitch*, Lord Worth, it would be six and half a dozen to me whether I was clobbered by shells or bombs. And planes could get away from the scene of the crime a damn sight faster than ships. They could get clean away. The US navy or land-based bombers would have a good chance of intercepting surface vessels. And another thing, Lord Worth.'

There was a moment's pause.

'A ship could stop at a distance of a hundred miles. No distance at all for the guided missile, I believe they have a range of four thousand miles these days. When the missile was, say, twenty miles from us, they could switch on its heat-source tracking device. God knows, we're the only heat-source for a hundred miles around.'

Another lengthy pause, then: 'Any more encouraging thoughts occur to you, Commander Larsen?'

'Yes, sir. Just one. If I were the enemy – I may call them the enemy – '

'Call the devils what you want.'

'If I were the enemy I'd use a submarine They don't' even have to break water to loose off a missile. Poof! No *Seawitch*. No signs of any attacker. Could well be put down to a massive explosion aboard the *Seawitch*. Far from impossible, sir.'

'You'll be telling me next that there'll be atomic-headed missiles.'

'To be picked up by a dozen seismological stations? I should think it hardly likely, sir. But that may just be wishful thinking. I have no wish to be vaporized.'

'I'll see you in the morning.' The line went dead.

Larsen hung up his phone and smiled widely. One would have subconsciously imagined this action to reveal a set of yellowed fangs: instead, it revealed a perfect set of gleamingly white teeth. He turned to look at Scoffield, his head driller and right-hand man.

Scoffield was a large, rubicund, smiling man, the easy-going essence of good nature. To the fact that this was not precisely the case any member of his drilling crews would have eagerly and blasphemously testified. Scoffield was a very tough citizen indeed and one could assume that it was not innate modesty that made him conceal this: much more probably it was a permanent stricture of the

33

facial muscles caused by the four long vertical scars on his cheeks, two on either side. Clearly he, like Larsen, was no great advocate of plastic surgery. He looked at Larsen with understandable curiosity.

'What was all that about?'

'The day of reckoning is at hand. Prepare to meet thy doom. More specifically, his lordship is beset by enemies.' Larsen outlined Lord Worth's plight. 'He's sending what sounds like a battalion of hard men out here in the early morning, accompanied by suitable weaponry. Then in the afternoon we are to expect a boat of some sort, loaded with even heavier weaponry.'

'One wonders where he's getting all those hard men and weaponry from.'

'One wonders. One does not ask.'

'All this talk – your talk – about bombers and sub-marines and missiles. Do you believe that?'

'No. It's just that it's hard to pass up the opportunity to ruffle the aristocratic plumage.' He paused then said thoughtfully: 'At least I hope I don't believe it. Come, let us examine our defences.'

'You've got a pistol. I've got a pistol. That's defences?'

'Well, where we'll mount the defences when they arrive. Fixed large-bore guns, I should imagine.'

'If they arrive.'

'Give the devil his due. Lord Worth delivers.'

'From his own private armoury, I suppose.'

'It wouldn't surprise me '

'What do you really think, Commander?'

'I don't know. All I know is that if Lord Worth is even half-way right life aboard may become slightly less monotonous in the next few days.'

The two men moved out into the gathering dusk on to the platform. The *Seawitch* was moored in 150 fathoms of water – 900 feet – which was well within the tensioning cables' capacities – safely south of the US's mineral leasing blocks and the great east-west fairway, straight on top of the biggest oil reservoir yet discovered round the shores of the Gulf of Mexico. The two men paused at the drilling derrick where a drill, at its maximum angled capacity, was trying to determine the extent of the oil-field. The crew looked at them without any particular affection but not with hostility. There was reason for the lack of warmth.

Before any laws were passed making such drilling illegal, Lord Worth wanted to scrape the bottom of this gigantic barrel of oil. Not that he was particularly worried, for government agencies are notoriously slow to act: but there was always the possibility that they might bestir themselves this time and that, horror of horrors, the bonanza might turn out to be vastly larger than estimated.

Hence the present attempt to discover the limits of the strike and hence the lack of warmth Hence the reason why Larsen and Scoffield, both highly gifted slave-drivers, born centuries out of their time, drove their men day and night. The men disliked it, but not to the point of re-bellion. They were highly paid, well housed and well fed. True, there was little enough in the way of wine, women and song but then, after an exhausting twelve-hour shift, those frivolities couldn't hope to compete with the attractions of a massive meal then a long, deep sleep. More importantly and most unusually, the men were paid a bonus on every thousand barrels of oil.

Larsen and Scoffield made their way to the western apex of the platform and gazed out at the massive bulk of the storage tank, its topsides festooned with warning lights. They gazed at this for some time, then turned and walked back towards the accommodation quarters.

Scoffield said: 'Decided upon your gun emplacements

35

vet, Commander - if there are any guns?'

'There'll be guns.' Larsen was confident. 'But we won't need any in this quarter.'

'Why?'

'Work it out for yourself. As for the rest, I'm not too sure. It'll come to me in my sleep. My turn for an early night. See you at four '

The oil was not stored aboard the rig – it is forbidden by a law based strictly on common sense to store hydrocarbons at or near the working platform of an oil rig. Instead, Lord Worth, on Larsen's instructions – which had prudently come in the form of suggestions – had had built a huge floating tank which was anchored, on a basis exactly similar to that of the *Seawitch* herself, at a distance of about three hundred yards. Cleansed oil was pumped into this after it came up from the ocean floor, or, more precisely, from a massive limestone reef deep down below the ocean floor, a reef caused by tiny marine creatures of a now long-covered shallow sea of anything up to half a billion years ago.

Once, sometimes twice a day, a 50,000 dw tanker would stop by and empty the huge tank. There were three of those tankers employed on the criss-cross run to the southern US. The Worth Hudson Oil Company did, in fact, have super-tankers, but the use of them in this case did not serve Lord Worth's purpose. Even the entire contents of the *Seawitch*'s tank would not have filled a quarter of the super-tanker's carrying capacity, and the possibility of a super-tanker running at a loss, however small, would have been the source of waking nightmares for the Worth Hudson: equally important, the more isolated ports which Lord Worth favoured for the delivery of his oil were unable to offer deep-water berth-side facilities for anything in excess of 50,000 dw.

It might in passing be explained that Lord Worth's choice of those obscure ports was not entirely fortuitous Among those who were a party to the gentlemen's agreement against offshore drilling – some of the most vociferous of those who roundly condemned Worth Hudson's nefarious practices - were, regrettably, Worth Hudson's best customers They were the smaller companies who operated on marginal profits and lacked the resources to engage in research and exploration, which the larger companies did, investing allegedly vast sums in those projects and then, to the continuous fury of the Internal Revenue Service and the anger of numerous Congressional investigation committees, claiming even vaster tax exemptions

But to the smaller companies the lure of cheaper oil was irresistible The *Seawitch*, which probably produced as much oil as all the government official leasing areas combined, seemed a sure and perpetual source of cheap oil until, that was, the government stepped in, which might or might not happen in the next decade: the big companies had already demonstrated their capacity to deal with inept Congressional enquiries and, as long as the energy crisis continued, nobody was going to worry very much about where oil came from, as long as it was there In addition, the smaller companies felt, if the OPEC – the Organization of the Petroleum Exporting Countries – could play ducks and drakes with oil prices whenever they felt like it, why couldn't they?

Less than two miles from Lord Worth's estate were the adjacent homes and common office of Michael Mitchell and John Roomer. It was Mitchell who answered the door bell

The visitor was of medium height, slightly tubby, wore wire-rimmed glasses and alopecia had hit him hard

He said: 'May I come in?' in a clipped but courteous enough voice.

'Sure.' Mitchell let him in. 'We don't usually see people this late.'

'Thank you. I come on unusual business. James Bentley.' A little sleight of hand and a card appeared. 'FBI.'

Mitchell didn't even look at it. 'You can have those things made at any joke shop. Where you from?'

'Miami.'

'Phone number?'

Bentley reversed the card which Mitchell handed to Roomer. 'My memory man. Saves me from having to have a memory of my own.'

Roomer didn't glance at the card either. 'It's okay, Mike. I have him. You're the boss man up there, aren't you?' A nod. 'Please sit down, Mr Bentley.'

'One thing clear, first,' Mitchell said. 'Are *we* under investigation?'

'On the contrary. The State Department has asked me to ask you to help them.'

'Status at last,' Mitchell said. 'We've got it made, John, but for one thing – the State Department don't know who the hell we are.'

'I do.' Discussion closed. 'I understand you gentlemen are friendly with Lord Worth.'

Roomer was careful. 'We know him slightly, socially - just as you seem to know a little about us.'

'I know a lot about you, including the fact that you are a couple of ex-cops who never learned to look the right way at the right time and the wrong way at the wrong time. Bars the ladder to promotion. I want you to carry out a little investigation into Lord Worth.'

'No deal,' Mitchell said. 'We know him slightly better than slightly '

'Hear him out, Mike.' But Roomer's face, too, had lost whatever little friendliness it may have held.

'Lord Worth has been making loud noises – over the phone – to the State Department. He seems to be suffering from a persecution complex. This interests the State Department, for they see him more in the role of the persecutor than the persecuted.'

'You mean the FBI does,' Roomer said. 'You'll have had him on your files for years. Lord Worth always gives the impression of being eminently capable of looking after himself.'

'That's precisely what intrigues the State Department.'

Mitchell said: 'What kind of noises?'

'Nonsense noises. You know he has an oil rig out in the Gulf of Mexico?'

'The *Seawitch*? Yes.'

'He appears to be under the impression that the *Seawitch* is in mortal danger. He wants protection. Very modest in his demands, as becomes a bulti-millionaire – the odd missile frigate, some missile fighters standing by, just in case.'

'In case of what?'

'That's the rub. He refused to say. Just said he had secret information – which, in fact, wouldn't surprise me. The Lord Worths of this world have their secret agents everywhere.'

'You'd better level with us,' Mitchell said.

'I've told you all I know. The rest is surmise. Calling the State Department means that there are foreign countries involved. There are Soviet naval vessels in the Caribbean at present. The State Department smells an international incident or worse.'

'What do you want us to do?'

'Not much. Just to find out Lord Worth's intended movements for the next day or two.'

39

Mitchell said: 'And if we refuse? We have our licences rescinded?'

'I am not a corrupt police chief. Just forget that you ever saw me. But I thought you might care enough about Lord Worth to help protect him against himself or the consequences of any rash action he might take. I thought you might care even more about the reactions of his two daughters if anything were to happen to their father.'

Mitchell stood up, jerked a thumb. 'The front door. You know too damn much.'

'Sit down.' A sudden chill asperity. 'Don't be foolish. Of course it's my job to know too damn much. But apart from Lord Worth and his family I thought you might have some little concern for your country's welfare.'

Roomer said: 'Isn't that pitching it a little high?'

'Very possibly. But it is the policy of both the State Department and the FBI not to take any chances.'

Roomer said: 'You're putting us in a damned awkward situation.'

'Don't think I don't appreciate that. Horns of a dilemma, torn loyalties, biting the hand that feeds you, all that sort of thing. I know I've put you in a spot and apologize for it, but I'm afraid you'll have to resolve that particular dilemma yourselves.'

Mitchell said: 'Thank you for dropping this little problem in our laps. What do you expect us to do? Go to Lord Worth, ask him why he's been hollering to the State Department, ask him what he's up to and what his immediate plans are?'

Bentley smiled. 'Nothing so crude. You have a re-markable reputation – except, of course, in the police department – of being, in that vulgar phrase, a couple of classy operators The approach is up to you.' He stood. 'Keep that card and let me know when you find out anything. How long would that take, do you think?'

Roomer said: 'A couple of hours.'

'A couple of hours?' Even Bentley seemed momentarily taken aback. 'You don't, then, require an invitation to visit the baronial mansion?'

'No.'

'Millionaires do.'

'We aren't even thousandaires.'

'It makes a difference. Well, thank you very much, gentlemen. Good night.'

After Bentley's departure the two men sat for a couple of minutes in silence, then Mitchell said: 'We play it both ways?'

'We play it every way.' Roomer reached for a phone. dialled a number and asked for Lord Worth. He had to identify himself before he was put through – Lord Worth was a man who respected his privacy.

Roomer said: 'Lord Worth? Mitchell and Roomer here Something to discuss with you, sir, which may or may not be of urgency and importance. We would prefer not to discuss it over the phone.' He paused, listened for a few moments, murmured a thank you and hung up.

'He'll see us right away. Park the car in the lane. Side door. Study. Says the girls have gone upstairs.'

'Think our friend Bentley will already have our phone tapped?'

'Not worth his FBI salt if he hasn't.'

Five minutes later, car parked in the lane, they were making their way through the trees to the side door. Their progress was observed with interest by Marina, standing by the window in her upstairs bedroom. She looked thoughtful for a moment, then turned and un-hurriedly left the room.

Lord Worth welcomed the two men in his study and securely closed the padded door behind them. He swung open the doors of a concealed bar and poured three brandies. There were times when one rang for Jenkins and there were times when one didn't. He lifted his glass.

'Health. An unexpected pleasure.'

'It's no pleasure for us,' Roomer said gloomily.

'Then you haven't come to ask me for my daughters' hands in marriage?'

'No, sir,' Mitchell said. 'No such luck. John here is better at explaining these things.'

'What things?'

We've just had a visit from a senior FBI agent.' Roomer handed over Bentley's card. 'There's a number on the back that we're to ring when we've extracted some information from you.'

'How very interesting.' There was a long pause then Lord Worth looked at each man in turn. 'What kind of information?'

'In Bentley's words, you have been making "loud noises" to the State Department. According to them, you seem to think that the *Seawitch* is under threat. They want to know where you got this secret information, and what your proposed movements are.'

'Why didn't the FBI come directly to me?'

'Because you wouldn't have told them any more than you told the State Department. If, that is to say, you'd even let them over the threshold of your house. But they know – Bentley told us this - that we come across here now and again, so I suppose they figured you'd be less off your guard with us.'

'So Bentley figures that you'd craftily wring some careless talk from me without my being aware that I was talking carelessly '

'Something like that '

'But doesn't this put you in a somewhat invidious position?'

42

'Not really.'

'But you're supposed to uphold the law, no?'

'Yes.' Mitchell spoke with some feeling. 'But not organized law. Or have you forgotten, Lord Worth, that we're a couple of ex-cops because we wouldn't go along with your so-called organized law? Our only responsibility is to our clients.'

'I'm not your client.'

'No.'

'Would you like me to be your client?'

Roomer said: 'What on earth for?'

'It's never something for nothing in this world, John. Services have to be rewarded.'

'Failure of a mission.' Mitchell was on his feet. 'It was kind of you to see us, Lord Worth.'

'I apologize.' Lord Worth sounded genuinely contrite. 'I'm afraid I rather stepped out of line there.' He paused ruminatively, then smiled. 'Just trying to recall when last I apologized to anybody. I seem to have a short memory. Bless my lovely daughters. Information for our friends of the FBI? First, I received my information in context of several anonymous threats – telephone calls – on the lives of my daughters. A double-barrelled threat, if you will – against the girls if I didn't stop the flow of oil - as they pointed out I can't hide them for ever and there's nothing one can do against a sniper's bullet – and if I were too difficult they'd have the *Seawitch* blown out of the water. As for my future movements, I'm going out to the *Seawitch* tomorrow afternoon and will remain there for twenty-four hours, perhaps forty-eight '

Roomer said: 'Any truth in either of those two statements?'

'Don't be preposterous. Of course not. I *am* going out to the rig - but before dawn. I don't want those beady-eyed bandits watching me from the undergrowth at my

43

heliport as I take off.'

'You are referring to the FBI, sir?'

'Who else? Will that do for the moment?'

'Splendidly.'

They walked back to the lane in silence. Roomer got in behind the wheel of the car, Mitchell beside him.

Roomer said: 'Well, well, well.'

'Well, as you say, well, well, well. Crafty old devil.'

Marina's voice came from the back. 'Crafty he may be, but – `

She broke off in a gasp as Mitchell whirled in his seat and Roomer switched on the interior lights. The barrel of Mitchell's .38 was lined up between her eyes, eyes at the moment wide with shock and fear

Mitchell said in a soft voice: 'Don't ever do that to me again. Next time it may be too late.'

She licked her lips. She was normally as high-spirited and independent as she was beautiful, but it is a rather disconcerting thing to look down the muzzle of a pistol for the first time in your life. 'I was just going to say that he may be crafty but he's neither old nor a devil. Will you please put that gun away? You don't point guns at people you love.'

Mitchell's gun disappeared. He said: 'I'm not much given to falling in love with crazy young fools.'

'Or spies.' Roomer was looking at Melinda. 'What are you two doing here?'

Melinda was more composed than her sister. After all, she hadn't had to look down the barrel of a pistol. She said: 'And you, John Roomer, are a crafty young devil. You're just stalling for time.' Which was quite true.

'What's that meant to mean?'

'It means you're thinking furiously of the answer to the same question we're about to ask you. What are *you* two doing here?'

'That's none of your concern.' Roomer's normally soft-spoken voice was unaccustomedly and deliberately harsh.

There was a silence from the back seat, both girls realizing that there was more to the men than they had thought, and the gap between their social and professional lives wider than they had thought.

Mitchell sighed. 'Let's cool it, John. Sharper than a serpent's tooth is an ungrateful child.'

'Jesus!' Roomer shook his head. 'That you can say again.' He hadn't the faintest idea what Mitchell was talking about.

Mitchell said: 'Why don't you go to your father and ask him? I'm sure he'll tell you – at the cost of the biggest shellacking you've ever had in your lives for interfering in his private business.' He got out, opened the rear door, waited until the sisters got out, closed the rear door, said 'Good night' and returned to his seat, leaving the sisters standing uncertainly at the side of the road.

Roomer drove off. He said: 'Very masterful, though I didn't like doing it. God knows, they meant no harm. Never mind, it may stand us in good stead in the future.'

'It'll stand us in even better stead if we get to the phone box just round the corner as soon as we can.'

They reached the booth in fifteen seconds and one minute later Mitchell emerged from it. As he took his seat Roomer said: 'What was all that about?'

'Sorry, private matter.' Mitchell handed Roomer a piece of paper. Roomer switched on the overhead light. On the paper Mitchell had scrawled 'This car bugged?'

Roomer said: 'Okay by me.' They drove home in silence. Standing in his carport Roomer said: 'What makes you think my car's bugged?'

'Nothing. How far do you trust Bentley?'

45

'You know how far. But he – or one of his men – wouldn't have had time.'

'Five seconds isn't a long time. That's all the time it takes to attach a magnetic clamp.'

They searched the car, then Mitchell's. Both were clean. In Mitchell's kitchen Roomer said: 'Your phone call?'

'The old boy, of course. Got to him before the girls did. Told him what had happened and that he was to tell them he'd received threats against their lives, that he knew the source, that he didn't trust the local law and so had sent for us to deal with the matter. Caught on at once. Also to give them hell for interfering.'

Roomer said: 'He'll convince them.'

'More importantly, did he convince you?'

'No. He thinks fast on his feet and lies even faster. He wanted to find out how seriously he would be taken in the case of a real emergency. He now has the preliminary evidence that he is being taken seriously. You have to hand it to him – as craftily devious as they come. Not that we haven't always known that. I suppose we tell Bentley exactly what he told us to tell him?'

'What else?'

'Do you believe what he told us to be the truth?'

'That he has his own private intelligence corps? I wouldn't question it for a moment. That he's going out to the *Seawitch?* I believe that, too. I'm not so sure about his timing, though. We're to tell Bentley that he's leaving in the afternoon. He told us he's leaving about dawn. If he can lie to Bentley he can lie to us. I don't know why he should think it necessary to lie to us, probably just his lordship's second nature. I think he's going to leave much sooner than that.'

Roomer said: 'Me, too, I'm afraid. If I intended to be up by dawn's early light I'd be in bed by now or heading that way. He shows no signs of going to bed, from which I can only conclude that he has no intentions of going to bed, because it wouldn't be worth his while.' He paused 'So. A double stake-out?'

'I thought so. Up by Lord Worth's house and down by his heliport. You for the heliport, me for the tail job?'

'What else?' Mitchell was possessed of phenomenal night-sight. Except on the very blackest of nights he could drive without any lights at all, an extraordinarily rare quality which, in wartime, made generals scour an army for such men as chauffeurs. 'I'll hole up behind the west spinney. You know it?'

'I know it. How about you feeding the story to Bentley while I make a couple of flasks of coffee and some sandwiches?'

'Fine.' Roomer reached for the phone, then paused 'Tell me, why are we doing all this? We owe nothing to the FBI. We have no authority from anyone to do anything. As you said yourself, we and organized law walk in different directions. I feel under no obligation to save my country from a non-existent threat. We have no client, no commission, no prospect of fees. Why should we care if Lord Worth sticks his head into a noose?'

Mitchell paused in slicing bread. 'As to your last question, why don't you ring up Melinda and ask her?'

Roomer gave him a long, old-fashioned look, sighed and reached for the telephone

chapter
3

Scoffield had been wrong in his guess. Lord Worth was possessed of no private armoury. But the United States armed services were, and in their dozens, at that.

The two break-ins were accomplished with the professional expertise born of a long and arduous practice that precluded any possibility of mistakes. The targets in both cases were government armouries, one army and one naval. Both, naturally, were manned by round-the-clock guards, none of whom was killed or even injured if one were to disregard the cranial contusions – and those were few – caused by sandbagging and sapping: Lord Worth had been very explicit on the use of minimal violence

Giuseppe Palermo, who looked and dressed like a successful Wall Street broker, had the more difficult task of the two, although, as a man who held the Mafia in tolerant contempt, he regarded the exercise as almost childishly easy. Accompanied by nine almost equally respectable men – sartorially respectable, that was – three of whom were dressed as army majors, he arrived at the Florida armoury at fifteen minutes to midnight. The six young guards, none of whom had even seen or heard a shot fired in anger, were at their drowsiest and expecting nothing but their midnight reliefs. Only two were really fully awake – the other four had dozed away – and those two, responding to a heavy and peremptory hammering on the main entrance door, were disturbed, not to say highly alarmed, by the appearance of three army officers who announced that they were making a snap inspection to test security and alertness. Five minutes later all six were bound and gagged – two of them unconscious and due to wake up with very sore heads because of their misguided attempts to put up a show of resistance – and safely locked up in one of the many so-called secure rooms in the armoury.

During this period and the next twenty minutes one of Palermo's men, an electronics expert called Jamieson, made a thorough and totally comprehensive search for all the external alarm signals to both the police and nearest military HQ. He either defused or disconnected them all.

It was when he was engaged in this that the relief guard, almost as drowsy as those whom they had been expecting to find, made their appearance and were highly disconcerted to find themselves looking at the muzzles of three machine-carbines. Within minutes, securely bound but not gagged, they had joined the previous guards, whose gags were now removed. They could safely shout until doomsday as the nearest place of habitation was over a mile away: the temporary gagging of the first six guards had been merely for the purpose of preventing their making loud noises and warning off their reliefs

Palermo now had almost eight hours before the break-in could be discovered.

He next sent one of his men, Watkins, to bring round to the front the concealed mini-bus in which they had arrived. All of them, Watkins excepted, changed from their conservative clothing and military uniforms into rough work clothes, which resulted in the effecting of rather remarkable changes in their appearance and character. While they were doing this Watkins went to the armoury garage, picked a surprisingly ineffectual

49

lock, selected a two-ton truck, wired up the ignition – the keys were, understandably, missing and drove out to the already open main loading doors of the armoury.

Palermo had brought along with him one by the name of Jacobson who, between sojourns in various penitentiaries, had developed to a remarkable degree the fine art of opening any type of lock, combination or otherwise. Fortunately, his services were not needed, for nobody, curiously enough, had taken the trouble to conceal some score of keys hanging on the wall in the main office.

In less than half an hour Palermo and his men had loaded aboard the truck – chosen because it was a covered-van type – a staggering variety of weaponry, ranging from bazookas to machine-pistols, together with sufficient ammunition for a battalion and a considerable amount of high explosives. This done, they locked all the doors they had unlocked and took the keys with them – when the next relief arrived at eight in the morning it would take them all that much longer to discover what had actually happened. After that, they locked the loading and main entrance doors.

Watkins drove the mini-bus, with its load of discarded clothes, back to its place of concealment, returned to the truck and drove off. The other nine sat or lay in varying degrees of discomfort among the weaponry in the back. It was as well for them that it was only twenty minutes' drive to Lord Worth's private, isolated and deserted heliport – deserted, that was, except for two helicopters, their pilots and co-pilots.

The truck, using only its sidelights, came through the gates of the heliport and drew up alongside one of the helicopters. Discreet portable loading lights were switched on, casting hardly more than a dull glow, but sufficient for a man only 80 yards away and equipped with a pair of night-glasses to distinguish clearly what was going on. And Roomer, prone in the spinney and with the binoculars to his eyes, was only 80 yards away. No attempt had been made to wrap or in any way disguise the nature of the cargo. It took only twenty minutes to unload the truck and stow its contents away in the helicopter under the watchful eye of a pilot with a keen regard for weight distribution.

Palermo and his men, with the exception of Watkins, boarded the other helicopter and sat back to await promised reinforcements. The pilot of this helicopter had already, as was customary, radio-filed his flight plan to the nearest airport, accurately giving their destination as the *Seawitch*. To have done otherwise would have been foolish indeed. The radar tracking systems along the Gulf states are as efficient as any in the world, and any deviation of course from a falsely declared destination would have meant that, in very short order, two highly suspicious pilots in supersonic jets would be flying alongside and asking some very unpleasant questions.

Watkins drove the truck back to the armoury garage, de-wired the ignition, locked the door, retrieved the mini-bus and left. Before dawn all his friends' clothes would have been returned to their apartments and the mini-bus, which had, inevitably, been stolen, to its parking lot.

Roomer was getting bored and his elbows were becoming sore. Since the mini-bus had driven away some half hour ago he had remained in the same prone position, his night-glasses seldom far from his eyes. His sandwiches were gone as was all his coffee, and he would have given much for a cigarette but decided it would be unwise. Clearly those aboard the helicopters were waiting for something and that something could only be the arrival of Lord Worth

He heard the sound of an approaching engine and saw another vehicle with only sidelights on turn through the gateway. It was another mini-bus. Whoever was inside was not the man he was waiting for, he knew: Lord Worth was not much given to travelling in mini-buses. The vehicle drew up alongside the passenger helicopter and its passengers disembarked and climbed aboard the helicopter. Roomer counted twelve in all.

The last was just disappearing inside the helicopter when another vehicle arrived. This one didn't pass through the gateway, it swept through it, headlights on but dipped. A Rolls-Royce. Lord Worth for a certainty. As if to redouble his certainty, there came to his ears the soft swish of tyres on the grass. He twisted round to see a car, both lights and engine off, coasting to a soundless stop beside his own

'Over here,' Roomer called softly. Mitchell joined him, and together they watched the white-clad figure of Lord Worth leave the Rolls and mount the steps to the helicopter. 'I should think that that completes the payload for the night.'

'The payload being?'

'There are twenty-one other passengers aboard that machine. I can't swear to it, but instinct tells me they are not honest, upright citizens. The story goes that every multi-millionaire – '

'Bulti.'

'Bulti. The story goes that every bulti-millionaire has his own private army. I think I've just seen one of Lord Worth's platoons filing by.'

'The second chopper plays no part in this?'

'Far from it. It's the star of the show. It's loaded to the gunwales with weaponry '

'Not a crime in itself. Could be part of Lord Worth's

private collection. He's got one of the biggest in the country.'

'Private citizens aren't allowed to have bazookas, machine-guns and high explosives in their collections.'

'He borrowed them, you think?'

'Yes. Without payment or receipt.'

'The nearest government armoury?'

'I should imagine.'

'They're still sitting there. Maybe they're waiting a pre-set time before take-off. Might be some time. Let's go to one of the cars and radio-phone the law.'

'The nearest army command post is seven miles from here.'

'Right.'

The two men were on their feet and had taken only two steps towards the cars when, almost simultaneously, the engines of both helicopters started up with their usual clattering roar. Seconds later, both machines lifted off.

Mitchell said: 'Well, it was a thought.'

' "Was" is right. And just look at them go. Honest God-fearing citizens with all their navigational lights on.'

'That's just in case someone bumps into them.' Mitchell thought. 'We could call up the nearest air force base and have them forced down.'

'On what grounds?'

'Stolen government property.'

'No evidence. Just our say-so. They'll have to know Lord Worth is aboard. Who's going to take the word of a couple of busted cops against his?'

'No one. A sobering thought. Ever felt like a pariah?'

'Like now. I just feel goddamned helpless. Well, let's go and find some evidence. Where's the nearest armoury from here?'

'About a mile from the command post. I know where.'

'Why can't they keep their damned armouries *inside*

53

their command posts?'

'Armouries can and do blow up. How would you like to be sitting in a crowded barracks when an armoury blew up?'

Roomer straightened from the key-hole of the main door of the armoury and reluctantly pocketed the very large set of keys for the carrying of which any ill-disposed law officer could have had him behind bars without any need for a warrant.

'I thought I could open any door with this little lot. But not this door. You don't have to guess where the keys are now.'

'Probably sailing down from a chopper in the Gulf.'

'Like as not. Those loading doors have the same lock. Apart from that, nothing but barred windows. You don't have a hacksaw on you, Mike?'

'I will next time.' He shone his torch through one of the barred windows. All he could see was his own reflection. He took out his pistol, and holding it by the barrel, struck the heavy butt several times against the glass, without any noticeable effect – hardly surprising considering that the window lay several inches beyond the bars and the force of the blows was minimal.

Roomer said: 'And just what are you trying to do?'

Mitchell was patient. 'Break the glass.'

'Breaking the glass won't help you get inside '

'It'll help me see and maybe hear. I wonder if that's just plate glass or armoured stuff?'

'How should I know?'

'True. Watch me finding out. If it's armoured, the bullet will ricochet. Get down.' Both men crouched and Mitchell fired one shot at an upward angle. The bullet did not ricochet. It passed through, leaving a jagged hole with radiating cracks. Mitchell began chipping away

54

round the hole but desisted when Roomer appeared with a heavy car jack: a few powerful blows and Roomer had a hole almost a foot in diameter. Mitchell shone his torch through this: an office lined with filing cabinets and an open door beyond. He put his ear as close to the hole as possible and he heard it at once, the faint but unmistakable sound of metal clanging against metal and the shouting of unmistakably hoarse voices. Mitchell withdrew his head and nodded to Roomer, who stooped and listened in turn.

Five seconds was enough. Roomer straightened and said: 'There are a lot of frustrated people in there.'

About a mile beyond the entrance to the army command post they stopped by a roadside telephone booth. Mitchell telephoned the army post, told them the state of defences at their armoury would bear investigation and that it would be advisable for them to bring along a duplicate set of keys for the main door. When asked who was speaking he hung up and returned to Roomer's car.

'Too late to call in the air force now, I suppose?'

'Too late. They'll be well out over extra-territorial waters by now. There's no state of war. Not yet.' He sighed. 'Why, oh why, didn't I have an infra-red ciné camera tonight?'

Over in Mississippi Conde's task of breaking into the naval armoury there turned out to be ridiculously easy He had with him only six men, although he had sixteen more waiting in reserve aboard the 120-foot vessel *Roamer* which was tied up dockside less than thirty feet from the armoury Those men had already effectively neutralized the three armed guards who patrolled the dock area at night.

The armoury was guarded by only two retired naval petty officers, who regarded their job not only as a sinecure

55

but downright nonsense, for who in his right mind would want to steal depth-charges and naval guns? It was their invariable custom to prepare themselves for sleep immediately upon arrival, and asleep they soundly were when Conde and his men entered through the door they hadn't even bothered to lock.

They used two fork-lift trucks to trundle depth-charges, light, dual-purpose anti-aircraft guns and a sufficiency of shells down to the dockside, then used one of the scores of cranes that lined the dockside to lower the stolen equipment into the hold of the *Roamer*, which was then battened down. Clearing the customs was the merest formality. The customs officials had seen the *Roamer* come and go so many times that they had long ago lost count. Besides, no one was going to have the temerity to inspect the ocean-going property of one of the richest men in the world: the *Roamer* was Lord Worth's seismological survey vessel.

At its base not far from Havana, a small, conventionally powered and Russian-built submarine slipped its moorings and quietly put out to sea. The hastily assembled but nonetheless hand-picked crew were informed that they were on a training cruise designed to test the sea-going readiness of Castro's tiny fleet. Not a man aboard believed a word of this.

Meanwhile Cronkite had not been idle. Unlike the others, he had no need to break into any place to obtain explosives. He just had to use his own key. As the world's top expert in capping blazing gushers he had access to an unlimited number and great variety of explosives. He made a selection of those and had them trucked down from Houston, where he lived – apart from the fact that Houston was the oil rig centre of the south the nature of his business made it essential for him to live within easy reach of an airport with international connections. They were then sent off to Galveston.

As the truck was on its way another seismological vessel, a converted coastguard cutter, was also closing in on Galveston. This vessel, without explaining his reasons why, Cronkite had obtained through the good offices of Durant, who had represented the Galveston area companies at the meeting of the ten at Lake Tahoe. The cutter, which went by the name of *Questar*, was normally based at Freeport, and Cronkite could quite easily have taken the shipment there, but this would not have suited his purpose. The tanker *Crusader* was unloading at Galveston and the *Crusader* was one of the three tankers that plied regularly between the *Seawitch* and the Gulf ports.

The *Questar* and Cronkite arrived almost simultaneously. Mulhooney, the *Questar*'s skipper, eased his ship into a berth conveniently close to the *Crusader*. Mulhooney was not the regular captain of the *Questar*. That gentleman had been so overcome by the sight of two thousand dollars in cash that he had fallen ill, and would remain so for a few days. Cronkite had recommended his friend, Mulhooney. Cronkite didn't immediately go aboard the *Questar*. Instead, he chatted with the chief customs inspector, who watched with an idle eye as what were obviously explosives were transferred to the *Questar*. The two men had known each other for years. Apart from observing that someone out in the Gulf had been careless with matches again, the customs official had no further pertinent comment to make.

In response to idle questioning Cronkite learned that the *Crusader* had just finished off-loading its cargo, and would be sailing in approximately one hour.

He boarded the *Questar*, greeted Mulhooney and went

57

straight to the crew's mess. Seated among the others there were three divers already fully clad in scuba suits. He gave brief instructions and the three men went on deck. Under cover of the superstructure and on the blind side of the ship – the side remote from the dock – the three men went down a rope ladder and slid quietly into the water. Six objects – radio-detonated magnetic mines equipped with metallic clamps – were lowered down towards them. They were so constructed as to have a very slight negative buoyancy, which made them easy to tow along under water.

In the pre-dawn darkness the hulls of the vessels cast so heavy a shadow from the powerful shorelights that it was virtually certain that the men could have swum unobserved on the surface. But Cronkite was not much given to taking any chances at all. The mines were attached along the stern half of the *Crusader*'s hull, thirty feet apart and set at a depth of about ten feet. Five minutes after their departure the scuba divers were back. After a further five minutes the *Questar* put out to sea.

Cronkite, despite his near-legendary reputation for ruthlessness, had not quite lost touch with humanity: to say that he was possessed of an innate kindliness would have been a distortion of the truth, for he was above all an uncompromising and single-minded realist, but one with no innate killer instinct. Nonetheless, there were two things that would at that moment have given him considerable satisfaction

The first of these was that he would have preferred to have the *Crusader* at sea before pressing the sheathed button before him on the bridge. He had no wish that innocent lives should be lost in Galveston, but it was a chance that he had to take. Limpet mines, as the Italian divers had proved in Alexandria in World War Two - and this to the great distress of the Royal Navy – could be devastatingly effective against moored vessels. But what might happen to high buoyancy limpets when a ship got under way and worked its way up to a maximum speed was impossible to forecast, as there was no known case of a vessel under way ever having been destroyed by limpet mines. It was at least possible that water pressure of a ship under way might well overcome the tenuous magnetic hold of the limpets and tear them free.

The second temptation was to board the helicopter on the *Questar*'s after helipad – many such vessels carried helicopters for the purpose of having them drop patterned explosives on the seabed to register on the seismological computer – and go to have a close look at what would be the ensuing havoc, a temptation which he immediately regarded as pure self-indulgence.

He put both thoughts from his mind. Eight miles out from Galveston he unscrewed the button-covered switch and leaned firmly on the button beneath. The immediate results were wholly unspectacular, and Cronkite feared that they might have been out of radio range. But for those in the port area in Galveston the results were highly spectacular. Six shattering explosions occurred almost simultaneously, and within twenty seconds the *Crusader*, her stern section torn in half, developed a marked list to starboard as thousands of tons of water poured through the ruptured side. Another twenty seconds later – making forty seconds in all – the distant rumble of the explosions reached the ears of the listeners on the *Questar*. Cronkite and Mulhooney, alone on the bridge – the ship was on automatic pilot – looked at each other with grim satisfaction. Mulhooney, an Irishman with a true Irishman's sense of occasion, produced an opened bottle of champagne and poured two brimming glassfuls. Cronkite, who normally detested the stuff, consumed his drink with considerable relish and set his glass down. It was then that the *Crusader* caught fire.

Its petrol tanks, true, were empty, but its engine diesel fuel tanks were almost completely topped up. In normal circumstances ignited diesel does not explode but burns with a ferocious intensity. Within seconds the smoke-veined flames had risen to a height of 200 feet, the height increasing with each passing moment until the whole city was bathed in a crimson glow, a phenomenon which the citizens of Galveston had never seen before and would almost certainly never see again. Even aboard the *Questar*, now some miles distant, the spectacle had an awe-inspiring and unearthly quality about it. Then, as suddenly as it had begun, the fire stopped as the *Crusader* turned completely over on its side, the harbour waters quenching the flames into hissing extinction. Some patches of floating oil still flickered feebly across the harbour, but that was all that there was to it.

Clearly, Lord Worth was going to require a new tanker, a requirement that presented quite a problem. In this area of a gross over-supply of tankers, any one of scores of laid-up super-tankers could be had just through exercising enough strength to lift a telephone. But 50,000-ton dw tankers, though not a dying breed, were a dwindling breed, principally because the main shipyards throughout the world had stopped producing them. 'Had' is the operative word. Keels of that size and even smaller were now being hastily laid down, but would not be in full operation for a year or two to come. The reason was perfectly simple. Super-tankers on the Arabian Gulf-Europe run had to make the long and prohibitively expensive circuit of the Cape of Good Hope because the newly reopened Suez Canal could not accommodate their immense draught, a problem that presented no difficulties to smaller tankers. It was said, and probably with more than a grain of truth, that the notoriously wily

Greek ship-owners had established a corner of this particular market.

The dawn was in the sky.

At that precise moment there were scenes of considerable activity around and aboard the *Seawitch*. The Panamanian registered tanker, the *Torbello*, was just finishing the off-loading of the contents of the *Seawitch*'s massive floating conical oil tank. As they were doing so, two helicopters appeared over the north-eastern horizon. Both were very large Sikorsky machines which had been bought by the thrifty Lord Worth for the traditional song, not because they were obsolete but because they were two of the scores that had become redundant since the end of the Vietnam war, and the armed forces had been only too anxious to get rid of them: civilian demand for ex-gunships is not high.

The first of those to land on the helipad debarked twenty-two men, led by Lord Worth and Giuseppe Palermo. The other twenty, who from their appearance were not much given to caring for widows and orphans, all carried with them the impeccable credentials of oil experts of one type or another. That they were experts was beyond question: what was equally beyond question was that none of them would have recognized a barrel of oil even if he had fallen into it. They were experts in diving, underwater demolition, the handling of high explosives and the accurate firing of a variety of unpleasant weapons.

The second helicopter arrived immediately after the first had taken off. Pilot and co-pilot apart, it carried no other human cargo. What it did carry was the immense and varied quantity of highly offensive weaponry from the Florida armoury, the loss of which had not yet been reported in the newspapers.

The oil rig crew watched the arrival of gunmen and

weapons with an oddly dispassionate curiosity. They were men to whom the unusual was familiar; the odd, the incongruous, the inexplicable, part and parcel of their daily lives. Oil rig crews were a race apart and Lord Worth's men formed a very special subdivision of that race.

Lord Worth called them all together, told of the threat to the *Seawitch* and the defensive measures he was undertaking, measures which were thoroughly approved of by the crew, who had as much regard for their own skins as the rest of mankind. Lord Worth finished by saying that he knew he had no need to swear them to secrecy

In this the noble lord was perfectly correct Though all experienced oilmen, there was hardly a man aboard who had not at one time or another had a close and painful acquaintanceship with the law. There were ex-convicts among them. There were escaped convicts among them. There were those whom the law was very anxious to interview. And there were parolees who had broken their parole. There could be no safer hideouts for those men than the *Seawitch* and Lord Worth's privately-owned motel where they put up during their off-duty spells No law-officer in his sane mind was going to question the towering respectability and integrity of one of the most powerful oil barons in the world, and by inevitable implication this attitude of mind extended to those in his employ.

In other words Lord Worth, through the invaluable intermediacy of Commander Larsen, picked his men with extreme care.

Accommodation for the newly-arrived men and storage for the weaponry presented no problem. Like many jack-ups, drill-ships and submersibles, the *Seawitch* had two complete sets of accommodation and messes, one for Westerners, the other for Orientals· there were at that time no Orientals aboard

Lord Worth, Commander Larsen and Palermo held

their own private council of war in the luxuriously equipped sitting-room which Lord Worth kept permanently reserved for himself. They agreed on everything. They agreed that Cronkite's campaign against them would be distinguished by a noticeable lack of subtlety: outright violence was the only course open to him. Once the oil was off-loaded ashore there was nothing Cronkite could do about it. He would not attempt to attack and sink a loaded tanker, just as he would not attempt to destroy their huge floating storage tank. Either method would cause such a massive oil slick, comparable to or probably exceeding the great oil slick caused by the Torrey Canyon disaster off the south-west coast of England some years previously. The ensuing international uproar would be bound to uncover something, and if Cronkite were implicated he would undoubtedly implicate the major oil companies – who wouldn't like that at all And that there would be a massive investigation was inevitable: ecology and pollution were still the watchwords of the day.

Cronkite could attack the flexible oil pipe that connected the rig with the tank, but the three men agreed that this could be taken care of. After Conde and the *Roamer* arrived and its cargo had been hoisted aboard, the *Roamer* would maintain a constant day-and-night patrol between the rig and the tank. The *Seawitch* was well equipped with sensory devices, apart from those which controlled the tensioning anchor cables. A radar scanner was in constant operation atop the derrick, and sonar devices were attached to each of the three giant legs some twenty feet under water. The radar could detect any hostile approach from air or sea, and the dual-purpose anti-aircraft guns, once aboard and installed, could take care of those. In the highly unlikely event of an underwater attack sonar would locate the source and a suitably placed depth-charge from the *Roamer* would attend to that.

Lord Worth, of course, was unaware that at that very moment another craft was moving out at high speed to join Cronkite on the *Questar*. It was a standard and well-established design irreverently known as the 'pull-push', where water was ducted in through a tube forward under the hull and forced out under pressure at the rear. It had no propeller and had been designed primarily for work close inshore or in swamps where there was always the danger of the propeller being fouled. The only difference between this vessel – the *Starlight* – and others was that it was equipped with a bank of lead acid batteries and could be electrically powered. Sonar could detect and accurately pinpoint a ship's engines and propeller vibrations: it was virtually helpless against an electric pull-push.

Lord Worth and the others considered the possibility of a direct attack on the *Seawitch*. Because of her high degree of compartmentalization and her great positive buoyancy nothing short of an atom bomb was capable of disposing of something as large as a football field. Certainly no conventional weapon could. The attack, when it came, would be localized. The drilling derrick was an obvious target, but how Cronkite could approach it unseen could not be imagined. But of one thing Lord Worth was certain: when the attack came it would be levelled against the *Seawitch*.

The next half hour was to prove, twice, just how wrong Lord Worth could be.

The first intimations of disaster came when Lord Worth was watching the fully-laden *Torbello* just disappearing over the northern horizon; the *Crusader*, he knew, was due alongside the tank late that afternoon. Larsen, his face one huge scowl of fury, silently handed Lord Worth a signal just received in the radio office. Lord Worth read it, and his subsequent language would have disbarred him for ever from a seat in the House of Lords. The message told, in cruelly unsparing fashion, of the spectacular end of the *Crusader* in Galveston.

Both men hurried to the radio room. Larsen contacted the *Jupiter*, their third tanker then off-loading at an obscure Louisiana port, told its captain the unhappy fate of the *Crusader* and warned him to have every man on board on constant look-out until they had cleared harbour.

Lord Worth personally called the chief of police in Galveston, announced who he was and demanded more details of the sinking of the *Crusader*. These he duly received and none of them made him any happier. On inspiration he asked if there had been a man called John Cronkite or a vessel belonging to a man of that name in the vicinity at the time. He was told to hang on while a check was made with the Customs. Two minutes later he was told yes, there had been a John Cronkite aboard a vessel called the *Questar*, which had been moored directly aft of the *Crusader*. It was not known whether Cronkite was the owner or not. The *Questar* had sailed half an hour before the *Crusader* blew up.

Lord Worth peremptorily demanded that the *Questar* be apprehended and returned to port and that Cronkite be arrested. The police chief pointed out that international law prohibited the arrest of vessels on the high seas except in time of war and, as for Cronkite, there wasn't a shred of evidence to connect him with the sinking of the *Crusader*. Lord Worth then asked if he would trace the owner of the *Questar*. This the police chief promised to do, but warned that there might be a considerable delay. There were many registers to be consulted.

At that moment the Cuban submarine steaming on the surface at full speed was in the vicinity of Key West and

65

heading directly for the *Seawitch*. At almost the same time a missile-armed Russian destroyer slipped its moorings in Havana and set off in apparent pursuit of the Cuban submarine. And, very shortly after that, a destroyer slipped its moorings at its home base in Venezuela.

The *Roamer*, Lord Worth's survey vessel under the command of Conde, was now half-way towards its destination. The *Starlight*, under the command of Easton, was just moving away from the *Questar*, which was lying stopped in the water. Men on stages had already painted out the ship's name, and with the aid of cardboard stencils were painting in a new name – *Georgia*. Cronkite had no wish that any vessel with whom they might make contact could radio for confirmation of the existence of a cutter called *Questar*. From aft there came the unmistakable racket of a helicopter engine starting up, then the machine took off, circled and headed south-east, not on its usual pattern-bombing circuit but to locate and radio back to the *Questar* the location and course of the *Torbello*, if and when it found it. Within minutes the *Questar* was on its way again, heading in approximately the same direction as the helicopter

chapter
4

Lord Worth, enjoying a very early morning cup of tea, was in his living-room with Larsen and Palermo when the radio operator knocked and entered, a message sheet in his hand. He handed it to Lord Worth and said: 'For you, sir. But it's in some sort of code. Do you have a code-book?'

'No need.' Lord Worth smiled with some little self-satisfaction, his first smile of any kind for quite some time. 'I invented this code myself.' He tapped his head. 'Here's my code-book.'

The operator left. The other two watched in mild anticipation as Lord Worth began to decode. The anticipation turned into mild apprehension as the smile disappeared from Lord Worth's face, and the apprehension gave way in turn to deep concern as reddish-purplish spots the size of pennies touched either cheek-bone. He laid down the message sheet, took a deep breath, then proceeded to give a repeat performance, though this time more deeply felt, more impassioned, of the unparliamentary language he had used when he had greeted the news of the loss of the *Crusader*. After some time he desisted, less because he had nothing fresh to say as from sheer loss of breath.

Larsen had more wit than to ask Lord Worth if something were the matter. Instead he said in a quiet voice: 'Suppose you tell us, Lord Worth?'

Lord Worth, with no little effort, composed himself and said· 'It seems that Cor – ' He broke off and corrected himself: it was one of his many axioms that the right hand shouldn't know what the left hand doeth. 'I was informed - all too reliably, as it now appears – that a couple of countries hostile to us might well be prepared to use naval force against us. One, it appears, is already prepared to do so. A destroyer has just cleared its Venezuelan home port and is heading in what is approximately our direction.'

'They wouldn't dare,' Palermo said.

'When people are power- and money-mad they'll stop at nothing.' It apparently never occurred to Lord Worth that his description of people applied, *in excelsis*, to himself

'Who's the other power?' said Larsen.

'The Soviet Union.'

'Is it now?' Larsen seemed quite unmoved 'I don't know if I like the sound of that.'

'We could do without them.' Lord Worth was back on balance again. He flipped out a telephone notebook and consulted it. 'I think I'll have a talk with Washington.' His hand was just reaching out for the receiver when the phone rang. He lifted the receiver, at the same time making the switch that cut the incoming call into the bulkhead speaker

'Worth.'

A vaguely disembodied voice came through the speaker. 'You know who I am?' Disembodied or not, Worth knew to whom the voice belonged. Corral

'Yes.'

'I've checked my contact, sir. I'm afraid our guesses were only too accurate. Both X and Y are willing to commit themselves to naval support.'

'I know. One of them has just moved out and appears to be heading in our general direction '

'Which one?'

'The one to the south. Any talk of air commitment?'

'None that I've heard, sir. But I don't have to tell you that that doesn't rule out its use.'

'Let me know if there is any more good news.'

'Naturally. Goodbye, sir.'

Lord Worth replaced the receiver, then lifted it again.

'I want a number in Washington.'

'Can you hold a moment, sir?'

'Why?'

'There's another code message coming through. Looks like the same code as the last one, sir.'

'I shouldn't be surprised.' Lord Worth's tone was sombre. 'Bring it across as soon as possible.'

He replaced the receiver, pressed a button on the small console before him, lifting the receiver as he did so.

'Chambers?' Chambers was his senior pilot.

'Sir?'

'Your chopper refuelled?'

'Ready to go when you are, sir.'

'May be any second now. Stand by your phone ' He replaced the receiver.

Larsen said: 'Washington beckons, sir?'

'I have the odd feeling that it's about to. There are things that one can achieve in person that one can't over the phone. Depends upon this next message.'

'If you go, anything to be done in your absence?'

'There'll be dual-purpose anti-aircraft guns arriving aboard the *Roamer* this afternoon. Secure them to the platform.'

'To the north, south, east but not west?'

'As you wish.'

'We don't want to start blowing holes in our own oil tank.'

'There's that. There'll also be mines. Three piles, each

half-way between a pair of legs.'

'An underwater explosion from a mine wouldn't damage the legs?'

'I shouldn't think so. We'll just have to find out, won't we? Keep in constant half-hourly touch with both the *Torbello* and the *Jupiter*. Keep the radar and sonar stations constantly manned. Eternal vigilance, if you will. Hell, Commander, I don't have to tell you what to do.' He wrote some figures on a piece of paper. 'If I do have to go, contact this number in Washington. Tell them that I'm coming. Five hours or so.'

'This is the State Department?'

'Yes. Tell them that at least the Under-Secretary must be there. Remind him, tactfully, of future campaign contributions. Then contact my aircraft pilot, Dawson. Tell him to be standing by with a filed flight plan for Washington.'

The radio operator knocked, entered, handed Lord Worth a message sheet and left. Lord Worth, hands steady and face now untroubled, decoded the message, reached for the phone and told Chambers to get to the helicopter at once.

He said to the two men: 'A Russian-built Cuban submarine is on its way from Havana. It's being followed by a Russian guided missile destroyer. Both are heading this way.'

'A visit to the State Department or the Pentagon would appear to be indicated,' Larsen said. 'There isn't too much we can do about guided missiles. Looks like there might be quite some activity hereabouts: that makes five vessels arrowing in on us – three naval vessels, the *Jupiter* and the *Roamer*.' Larsen might have been even more concerned had he known that the number of vessels was seven, and not five: but then Larsen was not to know that the *Questar* and the *Starlight* were heading that way also.

Lord Worth rose. 'Well, keep an eye on the shop. Back this evening some time. I'll be in frequent radio contact '

Lord Worth was to fly four legs that day: by helicopter to the mainland, by his private Boeing to Washington, the return flight to Florida and the final leg by helicopter out to the *Seawitch*. On each of those four legs something very unpleasant was going to happen – unpleasant for Lord Worth, that was. Fortunately for Lord Worth he was not blessed with the alleged Scottish second sight – the ability to look into the future.

The first of those unpleasantnesses happened when Lord Worth was en route to the mainland. A large estate wagon swept up to the front door of Lord Worth's mansion, carrying five rather large men who would have been difficult later to identify, for all five wore stocking masks. One of them carried what appeared to be a large coil of clothes rope, another a roll of adhesive tape. All carried guns.

MacPherson, the elderly head gardener, was taking his customary pre-work dawn patrol to see what damage the fauna had wreaked on his flora during the night when the men emerged from the estate wagon. Even allowing for the fact that shock had temporarily paralysed his vocal chords he never had a chance. In just over a minute, bound hand and foot and with his lips literally sealed with adhesive tape he had been dumped unceremoniously into a clump of bushes.

The leader of the group, a man by the name of Durand, pressed the front-door bell. Durand, a man who had a powerful affinity with banks and who was a three-time ex-convict, was by definition a man of dubious reputation, a reputation confirmed by the fact that he was a close and long-term associate of Cronkite. Half a minute passed then he rang again. By and by the door opened to reveal a robe-wrapped Jenkins, tousle-haired and blinking the sleep from his eyes – it was still very early in the morning. His eyes stopped blinking and opened wide when he saw the pistol in Durand's hand.

Durand touched the cylinder screwed on to the muzzle of his gun. As hooked a TV addict as the next man, Jenkins recognized a silencer when he saw one.

'You know what this is?'

A fully awake Jenkins nodded silently.

'We have no wish to harm anyone in this household. Especially, no harm will come to you if you do what you are told. Doing what you are told includes not telling lies Understood?'

Jenkins understood.

'How many staff do you have here?'

There was a noticeable quaver in Jenkins's voice. 'Well, there's me – I'm the butler – '

Durand was patient. 'You we can see.'

'Two footmen, a chauffeur, a radio operator, a secretary, a cook and two housemaids. There's a cleaning lady but she doesn't come until eight.'

'Tape him,' Durand said. Jenkins's lips were taped. 'Sorry about that, but people can be silly at times. Take us to those eight bedrooms.'

Jenkins reluctantly led the way. Ten minutes later all eight of the staff were securely bound and silenced. Durand said: 'And now, the two young ladies.'

Jenkins led them to a door. Durand picked out three of his men and said softly: 'The butler will take you to the other girl. Check what she packs and especially her purse.'

Durand, followed by his man, entered the room, his

gun in its concealed holster so as not to arouse too much alarm. That the bed was occupied was beyond doubt, although all that could be seen was a mop of black hair on the pillow. Durand said in a conversational voice: 'I think you better get up, ma'am.' Durand was not normally given to gentleness, but he did not want a case of screaming hysterics on his hands.

A case of hysterics he did not have. Marina turned round in bed and looked at him with drowsy eyes. The drowsiness did not last long. The eyes opened wide, either in fear or shock, then returned to normal. She reached for a robe, arranged it strategically on the bed cover, then sat bolt upright, wrapping the robe round her.

'Who are you and what do you want?' Her voice was not quite as steady as she might have wished.

'Well, would you look at that, now?' Durand said admiringly. 'You'd think she was used to being kidnapped every morning of her life.'

'This is a kidnap?'

'I'm afraid so.' Durand sounded genuinely apologetic.

'Where are you taking me?'

'Vacation. Little island in the sun.' Durand smiled. 'You won't be needing any swim-suit though. Please get up and get dressed.'

'And if I refuse?'

'We'll dress you.'

'I'm not going to get dressed with you two watching me.'

Durand was soothing. 'My friend will stand out in the corridor. I'll go into the bathroom there and leave the door open just a crack – not to watch you, but to watch the window, to make sure that you don't leave by it. Call me when you're ready and be quick about it.'

She was quick about it. She called him inside three minutes. Blue blouse, blue slacks and her hair combed.

Durand nodded his approval.

'Pack a travelling bag. Enough for a few days.'

He watched her while she packed. She zipped the bag shut and picked up her purse. 'I'm ready.'

He took the purse from her, unclipped it and up-ended the contents on the bed. From the jumble on the bed he selected a small pearl-handled pistol, which he slipped into his pocket.

'Let's pack the purse again, shall we?'

Marina did so, her face flushed with mortification.

A somewhat similar scene had just taken place in Melinda's bedroom.

Twenty-five minutes had elapsed since the arrival of Durand and his men and their departure with the two girls. No one had been hurt, except in their pride, and they had even been considerate to the extent of seating Jenkins in a deep armchair in the front hall. Jenkins, as he was now securely bound hand and foot, did not appreciate this courtesy as much as he might have done.

About ten minutes after their departure Lord Worth's helicopter touched down beside his Boeing in the city airport. There were no customs, no clearance formalities. Lord Worth had made it plain some years previously that he did not much care for that sort of thing, and when Lord Worth made things plain they tended to remain that way.

It was during the second leg of this flight that the second unfortunate occurrence happened. Again, Lord Worth was happily unaware of anything that was taking place.

The *Questar*'s (now the *Georgia*'s) helicopter had located the *Torbello*. The pilot reported that he had sighted the vessel two minutes previously and gave her latitude and

74

longitude as accurately as he could judge. More importantly, he gave her course as 315°, which was virtually on a collision course with the *Georgia*. They were approximately forty-five miles apart. Cronkite gave his congratulations to the pilot and asked him to return to the *Georgia*.

On the bridge of the *Georgia*, Cronkite and Mulhooney looked at each other with satisfaction. Between planning and execution there often exists an unbridgeable gap. In this case, however, things appeared to be going exactly according to plan.

Cronkite said to Mulhooney: 'Time, I think, to change into more respectable clothes. And don't forget to powder your nose.'

Mulhooney smiled and left the bridge. Cronkite paused only to give a few instructions to the helmsman, then left the bridge also.

Less than an hour later the *Torbello* stood clear over the horizon. The *Georgia* headed straight for it, then at about three miles' distance made a thirty degree alteration to starboard, judged the timing to a nicety and came round in a wide sweeping turn to port. Two minutes later the *Georgia* was on a parallel course to the *Torbello*, alongside its port quarter – the bridge of a tanker lies very far aft – paralleling its course at the same speed and not more than thirty yards away. Cronkite moved out on to the wing of the *Georgia*'s bridge and lifted his loud-hailer.

'Coastguard here. Please stop. This is a request, not an order. I believe your vessel to be in great danger. Your permission, please, to bring a trained search party aboard. If you value the safety of your men and the ship, on no account break radio silence.'

Captain Thompson, an honest sailor with no criminal propensities whatsoever, used his own loud-hailer.

'What's wrong? Why is this boarding necessary?'

75

'It's not a boarding. I am making a polite request for your own good. Believe me, I'd rather not be within five miles of you. It *is* necessary. I'd rather come aboard with my lieutenant and explain privately. Don't forget what happened to your sister ship, the *Crusader*, in Galveston harbour last night.'

Captain Thompson, clearly, had not forgotten and was, of course, completely unaware that Cronkite was the man responsible for what had happened to his sister ship: a ringing of bells from the bridge was indication enough of that. Three minutes later the *Torbello* lav stopped in the calm waters. The *Georgia* edged up alongside the *Torbello* until its midships were just ahead of the bulk of the tanker's superstructure. At this point it was possible to step from the *Georgia*'s deck straight on to the deck of the deeply-laden tanker, which was what Cronkite and Mulhooney proceeded to do. They paused there until they had made sure that the *Georgia* was securely moored fore and aft to the tanker, then climbed a series of companionways and ladders up to the bridge.

Both men were quite unrecognizable as themselves. Cronkite had acquired a splendidly bushy black beard, a neatly trimmed moustache and dark glasses and, with his neatly tailored uniform and slightly rakish peaked cap, looked the epitome of the competent and dashing coast-guard cutter captain which he was not. Mulhooney was similarly disguised.

There was only Captain Thompson and an unemployed helmsman on the bridge. Cronkite shook the captain's hand.

'Good morning. Sorry to disturb you when you are proceeding about your lawful business and all that, but you may be glad we stopped you. First, where is your radio room?' Captain Thompson nodded to a door set in back of the bridge. 'I'd like my lieutenant to check on the

radio silence. This is imperative.' Again Captain Thomp
son, now feeling distinctly uneasy, nodded. Cronkite
looked at Mulhooney. 'Go check, Dixon, will you?'

Mulhooney passed through into the radio room,
closing the door behind him. The radio operator looked
up from his transceiver with an air of mild surprise.

'Sorry to disturb.' Mulhooney sounded almost genial, a
remarkable feat for a man totally devoid of geniality.
'I'm from the coastguard cutter alongside. The captain
has told you to keep radio silence?'

'That's just what I'm doing.'

'Made any radio calls since leaving the *Seawitch*?'

'Only the routine half-hourly on course, on time calls.'

'Do they acknowledge those? I have my reasons for
asking.' Mulhooney carefully refrained from saying what
his reasons were

'No. Well, just the usual "Roger-and-out" business.'

'What's the call-up frequency?'

The operator pointed to the console. 'Pre-set.'

Mulhooney nodded and walked casually behind the
operator. Just to make sure that the operator kept on
maintaining radio silence, Mulhooney clipped him over
the right ear with the butt of his pistol. He then returned
to the bridge where he found Captain Thompson in a
state of considerable and understandable perturbation

Captain Thompson, a deep anxiety compounded by a
self-defensive disbelief, said: 'What you're telling me in
effect is that the *Torbello* is a floating time-bomb.'

'A bomb, certainly. Maybe lots of bombs. Not only
possible but almost certain. Our sources of information -
sorry, I'm not at liberty to divulge those - are as nearly
impeccable as can be '

'God's sake, man, no one would be so mad as to cause a
vast oilslick in the Gulf.'

Cronkite said: 'It's your assumption, not mine, that

77

we're dealing with sane minds. Who but a madman would have endangered the city of Galveston by blowing up your sister tanker there?'

The captain fell silent and pondered the question gloomily.

Cronkite went on: 'Anyway, it's my intention – with your consent, of course – to search the engineroom, living accommodation and every storage space on the ship. With the kind of search crew I have it shouldn't take more than half an hour.'

'What kind of pre-set time-bomb do you think it might be?'

'I don't think it's a time-bomb – or bombs – at all. I think that the detonator – or detonators – will be a certain radio-activated device that can be triggered off by any nearby craft, plane or helicopter. But I don't think it's slated to happen till you're close to the US coast '

'Why?'

'Then you will have the maximum pollution along the shores. There will be a national outcry against Lord Worth and the safety standards aboard his – if you will excuse me – rather superannuated tankers, perhaps resulting in the closing down of the *Seawitch* or the arrest of any of Lord Worth's tankers that might enter American territorial waters.' In addition to his many other specialized qualifications, Cronkite was a consummate liar. 'Okay if I call my men?' Captain Thompson nodded without any noticeable enthusiasm.

Cronkite lifted the loud-hailer and ordered the search party aboard. They came immediately, fourteen of them, all of them wearing stocking masks, all of them carrying machine-pistols. Captain Thompson stared at them in stupefaction then turned and stared some more at Cronkite and Mulhooney, both of whom had pistols levelled against him. Cronkite may have been looking satisfied or even triumphant, but such was the abundance of his ersatz facial foliage that it was impossible to tell

Captain Thompson, in a stupefaction that was slowly turning into a slow burn, said: 'What the hell goes?'

'You can see what goes. Hijack. A very popular pastime nowadays. I agree that nobody's ever hijacked a tanker before, but there always has to be someone to start a new trend. Besides, it's not really something new. Piracy on the high seas. They've been at it for thousands of years. Don't try anything rash, Captain, and please don't try to be a hero. If you all behave no harm will come to you Anyway, what could you possibly do with fourteen sub-machine-guns lined up against you?'

Within five minutes all the crew, officers and men, with one exception, were herded in the crew's mess under armed guard. Nobody had even as much as contemplated offering resistance. The exception was an unhappy-looking duty engineer in the engine room. There are few people who don't look slightly unhappy when staring at the muzzle of a Schmeisser from a distance of five feet.

Cronkite was on the bridge giving Mulhooney his final instructions.

'Continue sending the *Seawitch* its half-hourly on time, on course reports. Then report a minor breakdown in two or three hours – a fractured fuel line or something of the sort – enough that would keep the *Torbello* immobilized for a few hours. You're due in Galveston tonight and I need time and room to manoeuvre. Rather, *you* need time and room to manoeuvre. When darkness comes keep every navigational light extinguished - indeed, *every* light extinguished. Don't let's underestimate Lord Worth.' Cronkite was speaking with an unaccustomed degree of bitterness, doubtless recalling the day Lord Worth had taken him to the cleaner's in court 'He's an

79

exceptionally powerful man, and it's quite on the cards that he can have an air and sea search mounted for his missing tanker.'

Cronkite rejoined the *Georgia*, cast off and pulled away. Mulhooney, too, got under way, but altered course ninety degrees to port so that he was heading south-west instead of north-west. On the first half-hour he sent the reassuring report to the *Seawitch* – 'on course, on time'.

Cronkite waited for the *Starlight* to join him, then both vessels proceeded together in a generally south-eastern direction until they were about thirty-five nautical miles from the *Seawitch*, safely over the horizon and out of reach of the *Seawitch*'s radar and sonar. They stopped their engines and settled down to wait.

The big Boeing had almost halved the distance between Florida and Washington. Lord Worth, in his luxurious state-room immediately abaft the flight deck, was making up for time lost during the previous night and, blissfully unaware of the slings and arrows that were coming at him from all sides, was soundly asleep.

Mitchell had been unusually but perhaps not unexpectedly late in waking that morning. He showered, shaved and dressed while the coffee percolated, all the time conscious of a peculiar and unaccustomed sense of unease. He paced up and down the kitchen, drinking his coffee, then abruptly decided to put his unease at rest. He lifted the phone and dialled Lord Worth's mansion. The other end rang, rang again and kept on ringing. Mitchell replaced the receiver, then tried again with the same result. He finished his coffee, went across to Roomer's house and let himself in with his pass-key. He went into the bedroom to find Roomer still asleep. He woke him up. Roomer regarded him with disfavour.

'What do you mean by waking up a man in the middle of the night?'

'It's not the middle of the night.' He pulled open the drapes and the bright summer sunlight flooded the room. 'It's broad daylight, as you will be able to see when you open your eyes.'

'Is your house on fire or something, then?'

'I wish it were something as trivial as that. I'm worried, John. I woke up feeling bugged by something, and the feeling got worse and worse. Five minutes ago I called up Lord Worth's house. I tried twice. There was no reply. Must have been at least eight or ten people in that house, but there was no reply.'

'What on earth do you suppose –

'You're supposed to be the man with the intuition. Get yourself ready. I'll go make some coffee.'

Long before the coffee was ready, in fact less than ninety seconds later, Roomer was in the kitchen. He had neither showered nor shaved but had had the time and the grace to run a comb through his hair. He was looking the same way as the expressionless Mitchell was feeling.

'Never mind the coffee.' Roomer was looking at him with an almost savage expression on his face, but Mitchell knew that it wasn't directed at him. 'Let's get up to the house.'

Roomer drove his own car, which was the nearer.

Mitchell said: 'God, we're a bright lot. Hit us over the head often enough and then maybe – I only say maybe – we'll begin to see the obvious. But we're far too smart to see the obvious, aren't we?' He held on to his seat as Roomer, tyres screeching, rounded a blind corner. 'Easy, boy, easy. Too late to bolt the stable door now.'

With what was clearly a conscious effort of will Roomer slowed down. He said: 'Yes, we're the clever ones, Lord Worth offered as an excuse for his actions a threat of the

81

girls' abduction. You told him to offer the threat of the girls' abduction as an excuse for our presence there last night. And it never occurred to either of our staggering intellects that their abduction was both logical and inevitable. Lord Worth was not exaggerating – he has enemies, and vicious enemies who are out to get him, come what may. Two trump cards – and what trumps. All the aces in the pack. He's powerless now. He pretends to be loftily indulgent towards the two girls. He'll give away half his money to get them back. Just half. He'll use the other half to hunt them down. Money can buy any co-operation in the world, and the old boy *has* all the money in the world '

Mitchell now seemed relaxed, comfortable, even calm He said: 'But we'll get to them first, won't we, John?'

Roomer stirred uncomfortably in his seat as they swung into the mansion's driveway. He said: 'I'm just as sick and mad as you are. But I don't like it when you start to talk that way. You know that.'

'I should say I'm expressing an intention or at least a hope.' He smiled. 'Let's see.'

Roomer stopped his car in a fashion that did little good to Lord Worth's immaculately raked gravel. The first thing that caught Mitchell's eye as he left the car was an odd movement by the side of the driveway in a clump of bushes. He took out his gun and went to investigate, then put his gun away, opened his clasp-knife and sliced through MacPherson's bonds. The head gardener, after forty years in Florida, had never lost a trace of a very pronounced Scottish accent, an accent that tended to thicken according to the degree of mental stress he was undergoing. On this occasion, with the adhesive removed, his language was wholly indecipherable – which, in view of what he was almost certainly trying to say, was probably just as well in the circumstances

They went through the front doorway. Jenkins, apparently taking his ease in a comfortable armchair, greeted them with a baleful glare, a glare that was in no way directed at them. He was just in a baleful mood, a mood that was scarcely bettered when Mitchell, swiftly, painfully, and with scant regard for Jenkins's physical and mental feelings, yanked away the adhesive from his lips Jenkins took a deep breath, doubtless preparatory to lodging some form of protest, but Mitchell cut in before he could speak.

'Where does Jim sleep?' Jim was the radio operator.

Jenkins stared at him in astonishment. Was this the way to greet a man who had been through a living hell, snatched, one might almost say, from the jaws of death? Where was the sympathy, the condolences, the anxious questioning? Mitchell put his hands on his shoulders and shook him violently.

'Are you deaf? Jim's room?'

Jenkins looked at the bleak face less than a foot from his own and decided against remonstrating. 'In back, first floor, first right.'

Mitchell left. So, after a second or two, did Roomer. Jenkins called after him in a plaintive voice: 'You aren't leaving me too, Mr Roomer?'

Roomer turned and said patiently: 'I'm going to the kitchen to get a nice sharp carver. Mr Mitchell has taken the only knife we have between us.'

Jim Robertson was young, fresh-faced and just out of college, a graduate in electrical engineering in no hurry to proceed with his profession. He sat on the bed massaging his now unbound wrists, wincing slightly as the circulation began to return. As tiers of knots, Durand's henchmen had been nothing if not enthusiastic

Mitchell said: 'How do you feel?'

'Mad.'

83

'I shouldn't wonder. Fit to operate your set?'

'I'm fit for anything if it means getting hold of those bastards.'

'That's the general idea. Did you get a good look at the kidnappers?'

'I can give you a general description – ' He broke off and stared at Mitchell. 'Kidnappers?'

'It appears that Lord Worth's daughters have been abducted.'

'Holy Christ!' The assimilation of this news took some little time. 'There'll be all hell to pay for this.'

'It should cause a considerable furore. Do you know where Marina's room is?'

'I'll show you.'

Her room showed all the signs of a hasty and unpremeditated departure. Cupboard doors were open, drawers the same and some spilled clothing lay on the floor. Mitchell was interested in none of this. He quickly riffled through the drawers in her bedside table and within seconds found what he had hoped to find – a United States passport. He opened it and it was valid. He made a mental note that she had lied about her age – she was two years older than she claimed to be – returned the passport and hurried down to the radio room with Robertson, who unlocked the door to let them in. Robertson looked questioningly at Mitchell.

'The County Police Chief. His name is McGarrity. I don't want anyone else. Say you're speaking on behalf of Lord Worth. That should work wonders. Then let me take over.'

Roomer entered while Robertson was trying to make contact. 'Seven more of the staff, all suitably immobilized. Makes ten in all. I've left Jenkins to free them. His hands are shaking so badly that he's bound to slice an artery or two, but for me the freeing of elderly cooks and young housemaids lies above and beyond the call of duty.

'They must have been carrying a mile of rope,' Mitchell said absently. He was figuring out how much not to tell the chief of police.

Roomer nodded to the operator. 'Who's he trying to contact?'

'McGarrity.'

'That hypocritical old time-server.'

'Most people would regard that as a charitable description. But he has his uses.'

Robertson looked up. 'On the line, Mr Mitchell. That phone.' He made discreetly to replace his own but Roomer took it from him and listened in.

'Chief of Police McGarrity?'

'Speaking.'

'Please listen very carefully. This is extremely important and urgent, and the biggest thing that's ever come your way. Are you alone?'

'Yes. I'm quite alone.' McGarrity's tone held an odd mixture of suspicion and aroused interest.

'Nobody listening in, no recorder?'

'Goddam it, no. Get to the point.'

'We're speaking from Lord Worth's house. You know of him?'

'Don't be a damned fool. Who's "we"?'

'My name is Michael Mitchell. My partner is John Roomer. We're licensed private investigators.'

'I've heard of you. You're the pair who give the local law so much trouble.'

'I'd put it the other way round, but that's hardly relevant. What is relevant is that Lord Worth's two daughters have been kidnapped.'

'Merciful God in heaven!' There ensued what could fairly have been described as a stunned silence at the other end of the line.

Roomer smiled sardonically and covered his mouthpiece. 'Can't you see the old twister grabbing his seat, eyes popping, big signs saying "Promotion" flashing in front of him?'

'Kidnapped, you said?' McGarrity's voice had suddenly developed a certain hoarseness.

'Kidnapped. Abducted. Snatched.'

'Sure of this?'

'Sure as can be. The girls' rooms have every sign of a hurried unpremeditated departure. Ten of the staff bound and gagged. What would you conclude from that?'

'Kidnap.' McGarrity made it sound as if he'd made the discovery all by himself.

'Can you put a block on all escape routes? They haven't taken their passports, so that rules out international flights. I hardly think the kidnappers would have taken any commercial internal flight. Can you see Lord Worth's daughters passing through the crowded concourse of any terminal without being recognized? I suggest a stop order and permanent guard on every private airfield and heliport in the southern part of the state. And that goes for every port, big and small, in the same area.'

McGarrity sounded bemused, befuddled. 'That would call for hundreds of policemen.'

The tone of anguished protest was unmistakable. Mitchell sighed, cupped the mouthpiece, looked at Roomer and said: 'Man's out of his depth. Can I call him lunkhead?' He removed his hand. 'Look, Chief McGarrity, I don't think you quite realize what you're sitting on. It's the daughters of Lord Worth that we're talking about. You could lift your phone and have a thousand cops for the asking. You could call out the National Guard if you wanted – I'm sure Lord Worth would recoup every cent of expenses. Good God, man, there's been nothing like this since the Lindbergh kidnapping.'

'That's so, that's so.' It wasn't difficult to visualize McGarrity licking his lips. 'Descriptions?'

'Not much help there, I'm afraid. They all wore stocking masks. The leader wore gloves, which may or may not indicate a criminal record. All were big, well-built men and all wore dark business suits. I don't require to give you a description of the girls, I suppose?'

'Lady Marina? Lady Melinda?' McGarrity was a classic snob of awesome proportions, who followed with avid interest the comings and goings of alleged society, of the internationally famous and infamous. 'Good heavens, no. Of course not. They must be the most photographed couple in the State.'

'You'll keep this under wraps, tight as possible, for the moment?'

'I will, I will.' McGarrity had his baby clutched close to his heart, and nobody, but nobody was going to take it away from him.

'Lord Worth will have to be informed first of all. I'll refer him to you.'

'You mean you haven't told him yet?' McGarrity could hardly believe his good fortune

'No.'

'Tell him to rest easy, well, as easy as he can, that is. Tell him I'm taking complete and personal charge of the investigation.'

'I'll do that, Chief.'

Roomer winced and screwed his eyes shut.

McGarrity sounded positively brisk. 'Now, about the local law '

'I suppose I've got to call them in. I'm not too happy about it. They're biased against us Suppose they refuse to keep the wraps on this – '

'In which case,' McGarrity said ominously, 'just put the person concerned directly on the line to me Anyone else know about this yet?'

'Of course not. You're the only man with the power to authorize the closing of the escape routes. Naturally we contacted you first.'

'And you were perfectly right, Mr Mitchell.' McGarrity was warm and appreciative, as well he might have been, for he had a very shaky re-election coming up and the massive publicity the kidnapping was bound to generate would guarantee him a virtual shoe-in. 'I'll get the wheels turning this end. Keep me posted.'

'Of course, Chief.' Mitchell hung up.

Roomer looked at him admiringly. 'You are an even bigger and smarmier hypocrite than McGarrity.'

'Practice. Anyway, we got what we wanted.' Mitchell's face was sombre. 'Has it occurred to you that the birds may have flown?'

Roomer looked equally unhappy. 'It has. But first things first. Lord Worth next?' Mitchell nodded. 'I'll pass this one up. They say that, under provocation, he has a rich command of the English language, not at all aristocratic. I'd be better employed interviewing the staff. I'll ply them with strong drink to help them over-come the rigours of their ordeal and to loosen their tongues – Lord Worth's reserve Dom Perignon for choice – and see what I can extract from them. I have little hope. All I can ask them is about descriptions and voices and whether or not they touched anything that might yield up fingerprints. Not that that will help if their prints aren't on file.'

'The brandy sounds the best part of your programme. Would you ask Jenkins to bring a large one' – he looked at Robertson – 'two large ones?'

Roomer was at the door when he turned. 'Do you know what happened in ancient times to the bearers of bad news?'

'I know. They got their heads cut off.'

'He'll probably blame us for carelessness and lack of foresight – and he'll be right, too, even although he's just as guilty as we are.' Roomer left.

'Get me Lord Worth, Jim.'

'I would if I knew where he was. He was here last night when I left.'

'He's on the *Seawitch*.'

Robertson raised an eyebrow, lowered it, said nothing and turned his attention to the switchboard. He raised the *Seawitch* in fifteen seconds. Mitchell took the phone.

'Lord Worth, please.'

'Hold on.'

Another voice came on, a rasping gravelly voice, not as friendly.

'What is it that you want?'

'Lord Worth, please.'

'How do you know he's here?'

'How do I – what does that matter? May I speak to him?'

'Look, mister, I'm here to protect Lord Worth's privacy. We get far too many oddball calls from oddball characters. How did you know he was here?'

'Because he told me.'

'When?'

'Last night. About midnight.'

'What's your name?'

'Mitchell. Michael Mitchell.'

'Mitchell.' Larsen's tone had quite changed. 'Why didn't you say so in the first place?'

'Because I didn't expect a Gestapo investigation, that's why. You must be Commander Larsen?'

'That's me.'

'Not very bloody civil, are you?'

'I've a job to do.'

89

'Lord Worth.'

'He's not here.'

'He wouldn't lie to me.' Mitchell thought it impolitic to add that he'd actually seen Lord Worth take off.

'He didn't lie to you. He was here. He left hours ago to go to Washington.'

Mitchell was silent for a few moments while he readjusted himself. 'Has he got a number where he can be reached?'

'Yes. Why?'

'I didn't ask you why he'd gone to Washington. It's an urgent, private and personal matter. From what I've heard of you from Lord Worth, and that's quite a bit, you'd react in exactly the same way. Give me the number and I'll call you just as soon as Lord Worth gives me clearance.'

'Your promise?'

So Mitchell gave him his promise and Larsen gave him the number.

Mitchell replaced the receiver. He said to Robertson· 'Lord Worth has left the *Seawitch* and gone to Washington.'

'He does get around. In his Boeing, I presume?'

'I didn't ask. I took that for granted. Do you think you can reach him?'

Robertson didn't look encouraging. 'When did he leave the *Seawitch?*'

'I don't know. Should have asked, I suppose. Hours ago, Larsen said.'

Robertson looked even more discouraged. 'I wouldn't hold out any hope, Mr Mitchell. With this set I can reach out a couple of thousand miles. Lord Worth's Boeing can reach any airport not quite as far away, just as the airport can reach him. But the receiving equipment aboard the Boeing hasn't been modified to receive long-range transmissions from this set, which is a very specialized set indeed. Short-range only. Five hundred miles, if that. The Boeing is bound to be well out of range by now.'

'Freak weather conditions?'

'Mighty rare, Mr Mitchell.'

'Try anyway, Jim.'

He tried and kept on trying for five minutes, during which it became steadily more apparent that Lord Worth was going to have another brief spell of peace before being set up for his coronary. At the end of five minutes Robertson shrugged his shoulders and looked up at Mitchell.

'Thanks for the try, Jim.' He gave Robertson a piece of paper with a number on it. 'Washington. Think you can reach that?'

'That I can guarantee.'

'Try for it in half an hour. Ask for Lord Worth. Emphasize the urgency. If you don't contact him try again every twenty minutes. You have a direct line to the study?'

'Yes.'

'I'll be there. I have to welcome the law.'

Lord Worth, still happily unaware of his disintegrating world, slept soundly. The Boeing, at 33,000 feet, was just beginning its descent to Dulles airport.

chapter
5

Lord Worth, a glass of scotch in one hand and an illegal Cuban cigar in the other, was comfortably ensconced in a deep armchair in the Assistant Secretary of State's very plush office. He should have been contented and relaxed: he was, in fact, highly discontented and completely unrelaxed. He was becoming mad, steadily and far from slowly, at the world in general and the four other people in that room in particular.

The four consisted of Howell, the Assistant, a tall, thin, keen-faced man with steel-framed glasses who looked like, and in fact was, a Yale professor. The second was his personal assistant, whose name, fittingly enough, Lord Worth had failed to catch, for he had about him the grey anonymity of a top-flight civil servant. The third was Lieutenant-General Zweicker, and all that could be said about him was that he looked every inch a general. The fourth was a middle-aged stenographer who appeared to take notes of the discussion whenever the mood struck her which didn't appear to be very often: most likely, long experience had taught her that most of what was said at any conference wasn't worth noting anyway.

Lord Worth said: 'I'm a very tired man who has just flown up from the Gulf of Mexico. I have spent twenty-five minutes here and appear to have wasted my time. Well, gentlemen, I have no intention of wasting my time. My time is as important as yours. Correction. It's a damn sight more important. "The big brush-off" I believe it's called '

'How can you call it a brush-off? You're sitting in my office and General Zweicker is here. How many other citizens rate that kind of treatment?'

'The bigger the façade, the bigger the brush-off. I am not accustomed to dealing with underlings. I am accustomed to dealing with the very top, which I haven't quite reached yet, but will. The cool, diplomatic, deep-freeze treatment will not work. I am no trouble-maker, but I'll go to any lengths to secure justice. You can't sweep me under your diplomatic carpet, Mr Howell. I told you recently that there were international threats to the *Seawitch*, and you chose either to disbelieve me or ignore me. I come to you now with additional proof that I am under threat – three naval vessels heading for the *Seawitch* – and still you propose to take no action. And I would point out, incidentally, if you still don't know independently of the movements of those vessels, then it's time you got yourselves a new intelligence service.'

General Zweicker said: 'We are aware of those movements. But as yet we see no justification for taking any kind of action. You have no proof that what you claim is true. Suspicions, no more. Do you seriously expect us to alert naval units and a squadron of fighter-bombers on the unproven and what may well be the unfounded suspicions of a private citizen?'

'That's it in a nutshell,' Howell said. 'And I would remind you, Lord Worth, that you're not even an American citizen.'

Lord Worth, his voice gone very soft, pounced. ' "Not even an American citizen." ' He turned to the steno-grapher. 'I trust you made a note of that.' He lifted his hand as Howell made to speak. 'Too late, Howell. Too late to retrieve your blunder, a blunder, I may say, of classical proportions. Not an American citizen? I would point out that I paid more taxes last year than all your precious oil companies in the States combined - this apart from supplying the cheapest oil to the United States. If the level of competence of the State Department is typical of the way this country is run, then I can only rejoice in the fact that I still retain a British passport. One law for Americans, another for the heathen beyond the pale. Even-handed justice. "Not an American citizen " This should make a particularly juicy titbit for the news conference I intend to hold immediately after I leave.'

'A news conference?' Howell betrayed unmistakable signs of agitation.

'Certainly.' Lord Worth's tone was as grim as his face. 'If you people won't protect me then, by God, I'll protect myself.'

Howell looked at the General then back at Lord Worth. He strove to inject an official and intimidating note into his voice. 'I would remind you that any discussions that take place here are strictly confidential.'

Lord Worth eyed him coldly. 'It's always sad to see a man who has missed his true vocation. You should have been a comedian, Howell, not a senior member of government. Confidential. That's good. How can you remind me of something that you never even mentioned before? Confidential. If there wasn't a lady present I'd tell you what I really think of your asinine remark. God, it's rich, a statement like that coming from the number two in a Government department with so splendid a record of leaking State secrets to muck-raking journalists, doubtless in return for a suitable *quid pro quo*. I cannot abide hypocrisy. And this makes another juicy titbit for the press conference - the State Department tried to gag me. Classical blunder number two, Howell.'

Howell said nothing. He looked as if he were considering

the advisability of wringing his hands

'I shall inform the press conference of the indecision, reluctance, inaction, incompetence and plain running-scared vacillation of a State Department which will be responsible for the loss of a hundred million dollar oil rig, the stopping of cheap supplies of fuel to the American people, the biggest oil slick in history and the possible – no, I would say probable – beginnings of a third major war. In addition to holding this news conference, I shall buy TV and radio time, explain the whole situation and further explain that I am forced to go to those extraordinary lengths because of the refusal and inability of the State Department to protect me.' He paused. 'That was rather silly of me. I have my own TV and radio stations It's going to be such a burning hot topic that the big three companies will jump at it and it won't cost me a cent. By tonight I'll have the name of the State Department, particularly the names of you and your boss, if not exactly blackened at least tarnished across the country. I'm a desperate man, gentlemen, and I'm prepared to adopt desperate methods.'

He paused for their reactions. Facially they were all he could have wished. Howell, his assistant and the General all too clearly realized that Lord Worth meant every word he said. The implications were too horrendous to contemplate. But no one said anything, so Lord Worth took up the conversational burden again.

'Finally, gentlemen, you base your pusillanimous refusal to act on the fact that I have no proof of evil intent. I do, in fact, possess such proof, and it's cast-iron. I will not lay this proof before you because it is apparent that I will achieve nothing here. I require a decision-maker and the Secretary has the reputation for being just that. I suggest you get him here.'

'*Get* the Secretary?' Howell was clearly appalled by

this suggested lese-majesty. 'One doesn't "get" the Secretary. People make appointments days, even weeks in advance. Besides, he is in a very important conference.'

Lord Worth remained unmoved. 'Get him. This conference he'd better have with me will be the most important of his life. If he elects not to come then he's probably holding the last conference of his political career. I know he's not twenty yards from here. Get him.'

'I – I don't really think – '

Lord Worth rose. 'I hope your immediate successors – and the operative word is "immediate" - will, for the country's sake, display more common sense and intestinal fortitude than you have. Tell the man who, through your gross negligence and cowardly refusal to face facts, will be held primarily responsible for the outbreak of the next war, to watch TV tonight. You have had your chance – as your stenographer's notebook will show – and you've thrown it away.' Lord Worth shook his head, almost in sadness. 'There are none so blind as those who will not see – especially a spluttering fuse leading to a keg of dynamite. I bid you good day, gentlemen.'

'No! No!' Howell was in a state of very considerable agitation. 'Sit down! Sit down! I'll see what I can do.'

He practically ran from the room.

During his rather protracted absence – he was gone for exactly thirteen minutes – conversation in the room was minimal.

Zweicker said: 'You really mean what you say, don't you?'

'Do you doubt me, General?'

'Not any more. You really intend to carry out those threats?'

'I think the word you're searching for is "promises" '

After this effective conversation-stopper an uncomfortable silence fell on the room. Only Lord Worth appeared in no way discomforted. He was, or appeared to be, calm and relaxed, which was quite a feat, because he knew that the appearance or non-appearance of the Secretary meant whether he had won or lost

He'd won. The Secretary, John Belton, when Howell nervously ushered him in, didn't look at all like his reputation – which was that of a tough, shrewd-minded, hard-nosed negotiator, ruthless when the situation demanded and not much given to consulting his cabinet colleagues when it came to decision-making. He looked like a prosperous farmer, and exuded warmth and geniality – which deceived Lord Worth, a man who specialized in warmth and geniality, not a whit. Here, indeed, was a very different kettle of fish from Howell, a man worthy of Lord Worth's mettle. Lord Worth rose.

Belton shook his hand warmly. 'Lord Worth! This is a rare privilege – to have, if I may be forgiven the unoriginal turn of speech, to have America's top oil tycoon calling on us.'

Lord Worth was courteous but not deferential. 'I wish it were under happier circumstances. My pleasure, Mr Secretary. It's most kind of you to spare a few moments Well, five minutes, no more. My promise.'

'Take as long as you like.' Belton smiled. 'You have the reputation for not bandying words. I happen to share that sentiment.'

'Thank you.' He looked at Howell. 'Thirteen minutes to cover forty yards.' He looked back at the Secretary 'Mr Howell will have – ah · apprised you of the situation?'

'I have been fairly well briefed. What do you require of us?' Lord Worth refrained from beaming: here was a man after his own heart. John Belton continued. 'We can, of course, approach the Soviet and Venezuelan ambassadors, but that's like approaching a pair of powderpuffs. All they can do is to report our suspicions and veiled

97

threats to their respective governments. They're power-less, really. Even ten years ago ambassadors carried weight. They could negotiate and make decisions. Not any more. They have become, through no fault of their own, faceless and empty people who are consistently by-passed in State-to-State negotiations. Even their second chauffeurs, who are customarily trained espionage agents, wield more power than the ambassadors themselves.

'Alternatively, we can make a direct approach to the governments concerned. But for that we would have to have proof. Your word doesn't come into question, but it's not enough We must be able to adduce positive proof of, shall we say, nefarious intent.'

Lord Worth replied immediately. 'Such proof I can adduce and can give you the outline now. I am extremely reluctant to name names because it will mean the end of the professional career of a friend of mine. But if I have to, that I will do. Whether I release those names to you or to the public will depend entirely upon the Department's reaction. If I can't receive a promise of action after I have given you this outline, then I have no recourse other than to approach the public. This is not blackmail. I'm in a corner and the only solution is to fight my way out of it. If you will, as I hope you will, give me a favour-able reaction, I shall, of course, give you a list of names, which, I would hope, will not be published by your department. Secrecy, in other words. Not, of course, that this will prevent you from letting loose the FBI the moment I board my helicopter out there.'

'The great warm heart of the American public versus the incompetent bumbling of the State Department.' Belton smiled. 'One begins to understand why you are a millionaire – I do apologize, billionaire.'

'Earlier this week a highly secret meeting was held in a lakeside resort out west. Ten people, all of them very senior oilmen, attended this meeting. Four were Americans, representing many of the major oil companies in the States. A fifth was from Honduras. A sixth was from Venezuela, a seventh from Nigeria. Numbers eight and nine were oil sheikhs from the Gulf. The last was from the Soviet Union. As he was the only one there who had no interest whatsoever in the flow of oil into the United States, one can only presume that he was there to stir up as much trouble as possible.'

Lord Worth looked around the five people in the room. That he had their collective ear was beyond dispute. Satisfied, he continued.

'The meeting had one purpose and one only in mind. To stop me and to stop me at all costs. More precisely, they wanted to stop the flow of oil from the *Seawitch* – that is the name of my oil rig – because I was considerably undercutting them in price and thereby raising all sorts of fiscal problems. If there are any rules or ethics in the oil business I have as yet to detect any. I believe your congressional investigative committees would agree one hundred per cent with me on that. Incidentally, Worth Hudson – that's the official name of my company – has never been investigated.

'The only permanent way to stop the flow of oil is to destroy the *Seawitch*. Half-way through the meeting they called in a professional trouble-shooter, a man whom I know well, and a highly dangerous man at that. For reasons I won't explain until I get some sort of guarantee of help, he has a deep and bitter grudge against me. He also happens – just coincidentally, of course – to be one of the world's top experts – if not the very top – on the use of high explosives.

'After the meeting this trouble-shooter called aside the Venezuelan and Soviet delegates and asked for naval co-operation. This he was guaranteed.' Lord Worth looked

99

at the company with a singular lack of enthusiasm. 'Now perhaps you people will believe me.

'I would add that this man so hates me that he would probably do the job for nothing. However, he has asked for – and got – a fee of a million dollars. He also asked for – and got – ten million dollars "operating expenses". What does ten million dollars mean to you - except the unlimited use of violence?'

'Preposterous. Incredible.' The Secretary shook his head. 'It has, of course, to be true. You are singularly well-informed, Lord Worth. You would appear to have an intelligence service to rival our own.'

'Better. I pay them more. This oil business is a jungle and it's a case of the survival of the most devious.'

'Industrial espionage?'

'Most certainly not.' It was just possible that Lord Worth actually believed this.

'This friend who may be coming to the end of his

'Yes.'

'Give me all the details, including a list of the names. Put a cross against the name of your friend. I shall see to it that he is not implicated and that only I will see that list.'

'You are very considerate, Mr Secretary.'

'In return I shall consult with Defence and the Pentagon.' He paused. 'Even that will not be necessary. In return I can personally guarantee you a sufficiency of air and sea cover against any normal or even considerable hazard.'

Lord Worth didn't doubt him. Belton had the reputation of being a man of unshakeable integrity. More important, he had the justly-deserved reputation of being the President's indispensable right-hand man. Belton delivered. Lord Worth decided against showing too much relief.

'I cannot tell you how deeply grateful I am.' He looked at the stenographer, and then at Howell. 'If I could borrow this lady's services – '

'Of course.' The stenographer turned to a fresh page in her notebook and waited expectantly.

Lord Worth said: 'The place – Lake Tahoe, California. The address – '

The telephone jangled. The stenographer gave Lord Worth an 'excuse-me' smile and picked up the receiver. Howell said to the Secretary: 'Dammit, I gave the strictest instructions – '

'It's for Lord Worth.' She was looking at Belton. 'A Mr Mitchell from Florida. Extremely urgent.' The Secretary nodded and the stenographer rose and handed rest and receiver to Lord Worth.

'Michael? How did you know I was here? . . Yes, I'm listening.'

He listened without interruption. As he did so, to the considerable consternation of those watching him, the colour drained from his tanned cheeks and left them an unhealthy sallow colour. It was Belton himself who rose, poured out a brandy and brought it across to Lord Worth, who took it blindly and drained the not inconsiderable contents at a gulp. Belton took the glass from him and went for a refill. When he came back Lord Worth took the drink but left it untouched. Instead he handed the receiver to Belton and held his left hand over his now screwed-shut eyes.

Belton spoke into the phone. 'State Department. Who's speaking?'

Mitchell's voice was faint but clear. 'Michael Mitchell, from Lord Worth's home. Is that – is that Dr Belton?'

'Yes. Lord Worth seems to have received a severe shock.'

'Yes, sir. His two daughters have been kidnapped.'

'Good God above.' Belton's habitual imperturbability had received a severe dent. No one had ever seen him register shock before. Perhaps it was the bluntness of the announcement. 'Are you sure?'

'I wish to hell I wasn't, sir.'

'What are you?'

'We – my partner John Roomer and I – are private investigators. We are not here in an investigative capacity We are here because we are neighbours and friends of Lord Worth and his daughters '

'Called the police?'

'Yes.'

'What's been done?'

'We have arranged for the blocking of all air and sea escape routes.'

'You have descriptions?'

'Poor. Five men, heavily armed, wearing stocking masks.'

'What's your opinion of the local law?'

'Low.'

'I'll call in the FBI.'

'Yes, sir. But as the criminals haven't been traced there's no evidence that they've crossed the state line.'

'Hell with state lines and regulations. If I say they're called in, that's it. Hold on. I think Lord Worth would like another word.' Lord Worth took the receiver. Some colour had returned to his cheeks.

'I'm leaving now. Less than four hours, I should say. I'll radio from the Boeing half an hour out. Meet me at the airport.'

'Yes, sir. Commander Larsen would like to know – '

'Tell him.' Lord Worth replaced the receiver, took another sip of his brandy. 'There's no fool like an old fool and only a blind fool would have overlooked so obvious a move This is war, even if undeclared war, and in war no holds are barred. To think that it should come to this before you had incontrovertible proof that I am indeed under siege. Unforgivable. To have left my daughters unguarded was wholly unforgivable. Why didn't I have the sense to leave Mitchell and Roomer on guard?' He looked at his now-empty glass and the stenographer took it away.

Belton was faintly sceptical. '*Five* armed men?'

Lord Worth looked at him morosely. 'I had forgotten that you don't know these men. Mitchell, for example, could have taken care of them all by himself. He's lethal.'

'So they're your friends, and you respect them. Don't take offence, Lord Worth, but is there any way that they could be implicated in this?'

'You must be out of your mind.' Lord Worth, still morose, sipped his third brandy. 'Sorry. I'm not myself. Sure they'd like to kidnap my daughters, almost as much as my daughters would like to be kidnapped by them.'

'That the way?' Belton seemed mildly astonished. In his experience, billionaires' daughters did not normally associate with the lower orders.

'That's the way. And in answer to your next two questions: yes, I approve and no, they don't give a damn about my money.' He shook his head wonderingly. 'It is extremely odd. And I shall forecast this, Mr Secretary When Marina and Melinda are brought back to me it won't be through the good offices of either the local police or your precious FBI. Mitchell and Roomer will bring them back. One does not wish to sound overly dramatic, but they would, quite literally, give their lives for my daughters.'

'And, as a corollary, they would cut down anyone who got in their way?'

For the first time since the phone call Lord Worth smiled, albeit faintly. 'I'll take the fifth amendment on that one '

'I must meet these paragons some time.'

'Just as long as it's not over the wrong end of Mitchell's gun.' He rose, leaving his drink unfinished, looked round the room. 'I must go. Thank you all for your kindness and consideration, not to say forebearance.' He left, with the Secretary by his side.

When the door closed behind them General Zweicker rose and poured himself a brandy. 'Well. What may be the kidnapping of the century pales into insignificance compared to the likelihood of the Russkies starting to throw things at us.' He took some brandy. 'Don't tell me I'm the only person who can see the hellish witches' brew Lord Worth is stirring up for us.'

It was clear that all three listening to him had a very clear view of the cauldron. Howell said: 'Let's give Lord Worth his due. He could even be right when he says he's glad he's got a British passport. The stirrers-up are our own compatriots; the holier-than-thou major American oil companies, who are willing to crucify Lord Worth and put their country at jeopardy because of their blind stupidity.'

'I don't care who's responsible.' The stenographer's voice was plaintive. 'Does anyone know where I can get a nuclear shelter, cheap?'

Belton led Worth down one flight of stairs and out on to the sunlit lawn, where the helicopter was waiting.

Belton said: 'Ever tried to find words to tell someone how damnably sorry one feels?'

'I know from experience. Don't try. But thanks.'

'I could have our personal physician accompany you down to Florida.'

'Thanks again. But I'm fine now.'

'And you haven't had lunch?' Belton, clearly, was

finding conversational gambits heavy going.

'As I don't much care for plastic lunches from plastic trays, I have an excellent French chef aboard my plane.' Again a faint smile. 'And two stewardesses, chosen solely for their good looks. I shall not want.'

They reached the steps of the helicopter. Belton said· 'You've had neither the time, inclination nor opportunity to give me that list of names. For the moment that is of no consequence. I just want you to know that my guarantee of protection remains in force.'

Lord Worth shook his hand silently and climbed the steps

By this time Conde, aboard the *Roamer*, had arrived at the *Seawitch*, and the big derrick crane aboard the platform was unloading the heavy weaponry and mines from the Louisiana armoury. It was a slow and difficult task, for the tip of the derrick boom was 200 feet above sea level and in all the transfer was to take about three hours. As each dual-purpose anti-aircraft gun came aboard Larsen selected its site and supervised Palermo and some of his men in securing it in position: this was done by drilling holes in the concrete platform, then anchoring the gun-carriage base with sledge-hammer-driven steel spikes. The guns were supposed to be recoil-less, but then neither Larsen nor Palermo were much given to taking chances.

The depth-charges, when they came, were stacked together in three groups, each half-way between the three apexes of the triangle. That there was an inherent risk in this Larsen was well aware: a stray bullet or shell – or perhaps not so stray – could well trigger off the detonating mechanism of one of the depth-charges, which would inevitably send up the other charges in sympathetic detonation. But it was a risk that had to be taken if for no other reason than the fact that there was no other place where they could be stored ready for immediate use. And when and if the time came for their use the need would be immediate.

The drilling crew watched Palermo and his crew at work, their expressions ranging from dispassion to approval. Neither group of men spoke to the other. Larsen was no great believer in fraternization.

Things were going well. The defensive system was being steadily installed. The Christmas Tree, the peculiar name given to the valve which controlled the flow of oil from the already tapped reservoir, was wide open and oil was being steadily pumped to the huge storage tank while the derrick drill, set at its widest angle, was driving ever deeper into the sub-stratum of the ocean floor, seeking to discover as yet untapped new oil deposits. All was going well, there were no overt signs of attack or preparation for attack from air or sea, but Larsen was not as happy as he might have been, even despite the fact that they were still receiving the half-hour regular 'on course, on time' reports from the *Torbello*.

He was unhappy partly because of the non-existence of the *Questar*. He had recently learned from Galveston that there was no vessel listed in naval or coastguard registries under the name of *Questar*. He had then asked that they check civilian registrations and had been told that this was a forlorn hope. It would take many hours, perhaps days, to carry out this type of investigation and private vessels, unless fully insured, would show up neither in official registries nor in those of the major marine insurance companies. There was no law which said they had to be insured, and the owners of the older and more decrepit craft didn't even bother to insure: there are such things as tax write-offs.

Larsen was not to know that his quest was a hopeless one. When Mulhoonev had first taken over the *Questar* it had been called the *Hammond*, which he had thoughtfully had painted out and replaced by the name of *Questar* on the way to Galveston. Since Cronkite had since replaced that by the name *Georgia*, both the *Hammond* and the *Questar* had ceased to exist.

But what concerned Larsen even more was his conviction that something was far wrong. He was quite unable to put a finger on what this might be. He was essentially a pragmatist of the first order, but he was also a man who relied heavily on instinct and intuition. He was a man occasionally given to powerful premonitions, and more often than not those premonitions had turned into reality. And so when the loudspeaker boomed 'Commander Larsen to the radio cabin, Commander Larsen to the radio cabin,' he was possessed of an immediate certainty that the hour of his premonition had come

He walked leisurely enough towards the radio cabin, partly because it would never do for Commander Larsen to be seen hurrying anxiously anywhere, partly because he was in no great hurry to hear the bad news he was convinced he was about to hear. He told the radio operator that he would like to take this call privately, waited until the man had left and closed the door behind him, then picked up the telephone

'Commander Larsen.'

'Mitchell. I promised I'd call.'

'Thanks Heard from Lord Worth? He promised to keep in touch, but no word '

'And no wonder. His daughters have been kidnapped

Larsen said nothing immediately. Judging from the ivoried knuckles, the telephone handpiece seemed in danger of being crushed. Although caring basically only for himself, he had formed an avuncular attachment towards Lord Worth's daughters, but even that was unimportant compared to the implications the kidnapping held about the welfare of the *Seawitch*. When he did speak it was in a steady, controlled voice

'When did this happen?'

'This morning. And no trace of them. We've blocked every escape route in the southern part of the State. And there is no report from any port, airport, or heliport of any unusual departure from any of those since the time of the kidnapping.'

'Vanished into thin air?'

'Vanished, anyway. But not into thin air, we think. Terra firma, more likely. We think they've gone to earth, and are holed up not all that far away. But it's only a guess.'

'No communication, no demands, from the kidnappers?'

'None. That's what makes it all so odd.'

'You think this is a ransom kidnap?'

'No.'

'The *Seawitch?*'

'Yes.'

'Do you know why Lord Worth went to Washington?'

'No. I'd like to '

'To demand naval protection. Early this morning a Russian destroyer and a Cuban submarine left Havana, while another destroyer left Venezuela. They are on converging courses. The point of convergence would appear to be the *Seawitch*.'

There was a silence, then Mitchell said: 'This is for sure?'

'Yes. Well, Lord Worth's cup of woes would seem to be fairly full. The only consolation is that nothing much else can happen to him after this Please keep me informed.'

In Lord Worth's radio room both Mitchell and Roomer

hung up their phones.

Mitchell briefly indulged in some improper language. 'God, I never thought his enemies would go to this length.'

Roomer said: 'Neither did I. I'm not sure that I even think so now.'

'Uncle Sam's not going to let any foreign naval powers play ducks and drakes in his own backyard?'

'Something like that. I don't think the Soviets would go so far as to risk a confrontation. Could be a bluff, a diversionary move. Maybe the real attack is coming from elsewhere.'

'Maybe anything. Could be a double bluff. One thing's sure: Larsen's right in saying that Lord Worth's cup of woes is fairly full. In fact I'd say it was over-spilling.'

'Looks that way,' Roomer said absently. His thoughts were clearly elsewhere.

Mitchell said: 'Don't tell me you're in the throes of intuition again?'

'I'm not sure. When you were talking to Larsen just now you mentioned "terra firma". Firm land, dry land. What if it weren't dry land? What if it were *un*firm land?'

Mitchell waited politely.

Roomer said: 'If you wanted to hole up, really get lost in Florida, where would you go?'

Mitchell hardly had to think. 'We are bright. Unfirm land, infirm land, whatever you want to call it. The swamps, of course. Where else?'

'Man could hide out for a month there, and a battalion of troops couldn't find him. Which explains why the cops have been unable to find the station wagon.' Between them MacPherson and Jenkins had been able to give a fairly accurate description of the kidnappers' estate wagon. 'They've been checking the highways and byways.

I'll bet they never even thought of checking the roads into the swamps.'

'Did we?'

'As you said, we're bright. There are dozens of those roads into the swamps, but most of them are very short and in no time you reach a point where no wheeled vehicle can go any further. A few dozen police cars could comb the nearest swamps in an hour.'

Mitchell said to Robertson: 'Get Chief McGarrity.

A knock came on the half-open door and Louise, one of the young housemaids, entered. She held a card in her hand. She said: 'I was just making up Miss Marina's bed when I found this between the sheets.'

Mitchell took the card. It was a plain calling card giving Marina's name and address.

Louise said: 'Other side.'

Mitchell reversed the card, holding it so that Roomer could see. Handwritten with a ball-point were the words: 'Vacation. Little island in the sun. No swim-suit.'

'You know Miss Marina's handwriting, Louise?' Mitchell had suddenly realized that he didn't.

The girl looked at the card. 'Yes, sir. I'm sure.'

'Thank you, Louise. This could be very useful.' Louise smiled and left. Mitchell said to Roomer: 'What kind of lousy detective are you, then? Why didn't *you* think of searching the bedrooms?'

'Hmm. I can only guess that she asked them to leave while she dressed.'

'You'd have thought she'd have been too scared to think of this.'

'The handwriting's steady enough. Besides, she doesn't scare easily. Except, that is, when you point a pistol between her eyes.'

'I wish, right here and now, that I was pointing a pistol between someone else's eyes. Little island in the sun where you can't go bathing. An over-confident kidnapper can talk too much. You thinking what I'm thinking?'

Roomer nodded. 'The *Seawitch*.'

At 33,000 feet Lord Worth had just completed a light but delicious lunch accompanied by a splendid Bordeaux wine, specially bottled for him in a Rothschild vinery. He had regained his habitual calm. He was almost philosophical. He had, he reckoned, touched his nadir. All that could happen had happened. In common with Larsen, Mitchell and Roomer he was convinced that the Fates could touch him no more. All four were completely and terribly wrong. The worst was yet to come. It was, in fact, happening right then.

Colonel Farquharson, Lieutenant-Colonel Dewings and Major Breckley were not in fact the people their ID cards claimed they were, for the sufficient reason that there were no officers of that rank with corresponding names in the US army. But then it was a very big army, and nobody, not even the officers, could possibly be expected to know the names of more than a tiny fraction of their fellow officers. Nor were their faces their normal faces, although they could hardly be described as being heavily disguised. The man responsible had been a Hollywood make-up artist who preferred subtlety to false beards. All three men were dressed in sober and well-cut business suits.

Farquharson presented his card to the corporal at the outer reception desk. 'Colonel Farquharson to see Colonel Pryce.'

'I'm afraid he's not here.

'Then the officer in charge, man.

'Yes, sir.'

A minute later they were seated before a young and apprehensive Captain Martin, who had just finished a

rather reluctant and very perfunctory scrutiny of their
ID cards.

Farquharson said: 'So Colonel Pryce has been called to
Washington. I can guess why.'

He didn't have to guess. He himself had put through
the fake call that had led to Pryce's abrupt departure
'And his second in command?'

'Flu.' Martin sounded apologetic

'At this time of year? How inconvenient Especially
today. You can guess why we're here '

'Yes, sir.' Martin looked slightly unhappy. 'Security
check. I had a phone call telling me of the break-ins into
the Florida and Louisiana armouries.' Dewings had put
through that one. 'I'm sure you'll find everything in
order.'

'Doubtless. I have already discovered something that
is not in order '

'Sir?' There was a definite apprehension now in
Martin's voice and appearance.

'Security-consciousness. Do you know that there are
literally dozens of shops where I could buy, perfectly
legally, a general's uniform? Those are the speciality
shops that cater primarily for the film and stage industries.
If I walked in dressed in such a uniform, would you
accept me for what my uniform proclaimed me to be?'

'I suppose I would, sir.'

'Well, don't. Not ever again.' He glanced at his identity
card lying on the desk. 'Forging one of those presents no
problems. When a stranger makes an appearance in a
top-security place like this, always, *always*, check his
identity with Area Command. And always talk only to
the commanding officer.'

'Yes, sir. Do you happen to know his name? I'm new
here '

'Major-General Harsworth '

Martin had the corporal at the front desk put him through. On the first ring a voice answered 'Area Command '

The voice did not in fact come from Area Command. It came from a man less than half a mile away, seated at the base of a telegraph pole. He had with him a battery-powered transceiver. A sheathed copper line from that led up to a crocodile clip attached to one of the telegraph lines.

Martin said: 'Netley Rowan Armoury. Captain Martin J'd like to speak to General Harsworth.'

'Hold.' There was a series of clicks, a pause of some seconds, then the same voice said: 'On the line, Captain.'

Martin said: 'General Harsworth?'

'Speaking.' The man by the telegraph pole had deepened his voice by an octave. 'Problems, Captain Martin?'

'I have Colonel Farquharson with me. He insists that I check out his identity with you.'

The voice at the other end was sympathetic. 'Been at the receiving end of a security lecture?'

'I'm afraid I have rather, sir.'

'Very hot on security, the Colonel. He'll be with Lieutenant-Colonel Dewings and Major Breckley?'

'Yes, sir.'

'Well, it's hardly the end of your professional career. But he's right, you know.'

Farquharson himself took the wheel of the car on the three-mile journey, a chastened, compliant Martin sitting up front beside him. A fifteen-foot-high electrical warning barbed-wire fence surrounded the armoury, a squat, grey, windowless building covering almost half an acre of land. A sentry with a machine-carbine barred the entrance to the compound. He recognized Captain Martin, stepped back and saluted. Farquharson drove up to the one and only door of the armoury and halted. The four men got out. Farquharson said to Martin: 'Major Breckley has never been inside a TNW armoury before. A few illuminating comments, perhaps?' It would be illuminating for Farquharson also. He had never been inside an armoury of any description in his life.

'Yes, sir. TNW – Tactical Nuclear Warfare. Walls thirty-three inches thick, alternating steel and ferroconcrete. Door – ten inches tungsten steel. Both walls and door capable of resisting the equivalent of a fourteen-inch armour-piercing naval shell. This glass panel is recording us on TV videotape. This meshed grille is a two-way speaker which also records our voices.' He pressed a button sunk in the concrete.

A voice came through the grille. 'Identification, please?'

'Captain Martin with Colonel Farquharson and security inspection.'

'Code?'

'Geronimo.' The massive door began to slide open, and they could hear the hum of a powerful electrical motor. It took all of ten seconds for the door to open to its fullest extent. Martin led them inside.

A corporal saluted their entrance. Martin said: 'Security inspection tour.'

'Yes, sir.' The corporal didn't seem too happy.

Farquharson said: 'You seem to have a troubled conscience, soldier?'

'No, sir.'

'Then you should have.'

Martin said: 'Something wrong, sir?' He was patently nervous.

'Four things.' Martin dipped his head so that Farquharson couldn't see that he had been swallowing. One thing would have been bad enough.

'In the first place, that sentry gate should be kept

permanently locked. It should only be opened after a phone call to your HQ and an electronic link for opening the gate installed in your office. What's to prevent a person or persons with a silenced automatic disposing of your sentry and driving straight up here? Secondly, what would prevent such people walking through the open doorway and riddling us all with sub-machine-guns? That door should have been shut the moment we passed through.' The corporal started to move but Farquharson stopped him with upraised hand.

'Thirdly, all people who are not base personnel – such as us – should be finger-printed on arrival – I will arrange to have your guards trained in those techniques. Fourthly, and most importantly, show me the controls for those doors.'

'This way, sir.' The corporal led the way to a small console. 'The red button opens, the green one closes.'

Farquharson pressed the green button. The massive door hissed slowly closed. 'Unsatisfactory. Totally Those are the only controls to operate the door?'

'Yes, sir.' Martin looked very unhappy indeed.

'We shall have another electronic link established with your HQ, which will render those buttons inoperable until the correct signal is sent.' Farquharson was showing signs of irritation. 'I would have thought all those things were self-evident.'

Martin smiled weakly. 'They are now, sir.'

'What percentage of explosives, bombs and shells stored here are conventional?'

'Close on ninety-five per cent, sir.'

'I'd like to see the nuclear weapons first.'

'Of course, sir.' A now thoroughly demoralized Martin led the way.

The TNW section was compartmented off but not sealed. One side was lined with what appeared to be shells, stowed on racks, the other with pear-shaped metal canisters about thirty inches high, with buttons, a clock-face and a large knurled screw on top. Beyond them were stacked what looked like very odd-shaped fibre-glass suitcases, each with two leather handles.

Breckley indicated the pear-shaped canisters. 'What are those? Bombs?'

'Both bombs and landmines.' Martin seemed glad to talk and take his mind off his troubles. 'Those controls on top are relatively simple. Before you get at those two red switches you have to unscrew those two transparent plastic covers. The switches have then to be turned ninety degrees to the right. They are then still in the safe position. They then have to be flipped ninety degrees to the left. This is the ready-to-activate position.

'Before that is done, you have to put the time setting on the clock. That is done by means of this knurled knob here. One complete turn means a one-minute time delay which will show up on this clock face here. It registers in seconds, as you can see. Total time delay is thirty minutes – thirty turns.'

'And this black button?'

'The most important of them all. No cover and no turning. You might want to get at it in a hurry Depressing that stops the clock and, in fact, deactivates the bomb.'

'What's the area of damage?'

'Compared to the conventional atom bomb, tiny. The vaporization area would be a quarter-mile radius. Perhaps less. The blast, shock and radiation areas would, of course, be considerably greater.'

'You said they could be used as both bombs and mines.'

'For mines I should perhaps have said an explosive device for use on land. As bombs the setting would probably be only six seconds – in tactical warfare they would be carried by low-flying supersonic planes. They'd be about two miles clear by the time the bomb went off and moving too fast for the shock waves to catch up with them. For land use – well, say you wanted to infiltrate an ammunition dump. You'd check how long it would take you to infiltrate there, calculate how long it would take you to get out and clear of the blast zone and set the timer accordingly

'The missiles here - '

We've seen and heard enough,' Farquharson said 'Kindly put your hands up '

Five minutes later, with furiously reluctant assistance from Martin, they had loaded two bombs, safely concealed in their carrying-cases, into the trunk of their car. In so doing the need of the two carrying handles became clear. each bomb must have weighed at least ninety pounds

Farquharson went back inside, looked indifferently at the two bound men, pressed the button and slipped through the doorway as the door began to close. He waited until the door was completely shut, then climbed into the front seat beside Martin, who was at the wheel this time. Farquharson said: 'Remember, one false move and you're a dead man. We will, of course, have to kill the sentry too.'

There were no false moves About a mile from the armoury the car stopped by a thicket of stunted trees Martin was marched deep into the thicket. bound. gagged and attached to a tree just in case he might have any ideas about jack-knifing his way down to the roadside. Farquharson looked down at him.

'Your security *was* lousy. We'll phone your HQ in an hour or so, let them know where they can find you I trust there are not too many rattlesnakes around '

chapter

Robertson looked up from the radio console 'Chief McGarrity'

Mitchell took the phone. 'Mitchell? We've found the kidnappers' estate wagon. Down by the Wyanee swamp.' McGarrity sounded positively elated. 'I'm going there personally. Tracker dogs. I'll wait for you at the Walnut Tree crossing.' Mitchell replaced the receiver and said to Roomer. 'McGarrity's got it all wrapped up. He's found the estate wagon. Well, someone else did, but it will be made clear eventually that McGarrity did.'

'Empty, of course. Doesn't that old fool know that this makes it more difficult, not easier? At least we knew what transport they were using. Not any more. He didn't mention anything about bringing along a newspaper photographer that he just sort of accidentally bumped into?'

'Tracker dogs were all he mentioned.'

'Did he suggest source material for the dogs to sniff at?' Mitchell shook his head, Roomer shook his and after a few minutes Jenkins appeared. 'Will you get Louise, please?'

Louise appeared very quickly Roomer said. 'We'd like an article, a piece of clothing, that the ladies used to wear a lot'

She looked uncertain 'I don't understand -

'Some things we can give bloodhounds to sniff so that

they pick up the scent.'

'Oh.' It required only a second's thought. 'Their dressing-gowns, of course.' This with but the slightest hint of disapproval, as if the girls spent most of the day lounging about in those garments.

'Handle as little as possible, please. Put each in a separate plastic bag.'

A police car and a small closed police van awaited them at the Walnut Tree crossing. McGarrity was standing by the police car. He was a small bouncy man who radiated bonhomie and who only stopped smiling when he vehemently denounced corruption in politics. He was a police chief of incomparable incompetence, but was a consummate and wholly corrupt politician, which was why he was police chief. He shook the hands of Mitchell and Roomer with all the warmth and sincerity of an incumbent coming up for re-election, which was precisely what he was.

'Glad to meet you two gentlemen at last. Heard very good reports about you.' He appeared to have conveniently forgotten his allegation that they gave a lot of trouble to the local law Appreciate all the co-operation you've given me – and for turning up here now. This is Ron Stewart of the *Herald*.' He gestured through an open car window where a man, apparently festooned in cameras, sat in the back seat. 'Kind of accidentally bumped into him.'

Mitchell choked, turning it into a cough. 'Too many cigarettes.'

'Same failing myself. Driver's the dog-handler. Driver of the van is the other one. Just follow us, please.'

Five miles further on they reached the turn-off – one of many – into the Wyanee swamp. The foliage of the trees, almost touching overhead, quickly reduced the light to that of a late winter afternoon. The increase in the humidity was almost immediately noticeable, as was the sour nose-wrinkling miasma as they neared the swamps. A distinctly unhealthy atmosphere, or such was the first impression: but many people with a marked aversion to what passed for civilization lived there all their lives and seemed none the worse for it.

The increasingly rutted, bumpy road had become almost intolerable until they rounded a blind corner and came across the abandoned station wagon.

The first essential was, apparently, that pictures be taken, and the second that McGarrity be well-placed in each one, his hand, for preference, resting in a proprietorial fashion on the hood. That done, the cameraman fitted a flashlight and was reaching for the rear door when Roomer clamped his wrist not too gently. 'Don't do that!'

'Why not?'

'Never been on a criminal case before? Fingerprints is why not.' He looked at McGarrity. 'Expecting them soon?'

'Shouldn't be long. Out on a case. Check on them, Don.' This to the driver who immediately got busy on his radio. It was clear that the idea of bringing fingerprint experts along had never occurred to McGarrity.

The dogs were released from the van. Roomer and Mitchell opened up their plastic bags and allowed the dogs to sniff the dressing-gowns. McGarrity said: 'What you got there?'

'The girls' dressing-gowns. To give your hounds a trace. We knew you'd want something.'

'Of course. But dressing-gowns!' McGarrity was a past master in covering up. Something else, clearly, that had not occurred to him.

The dogs caught the scents at once and strained at their leashes as they nosed their way down a rutted path, for the road had come to an abrupt end. Inside a hundred yards, their path was blocked by water. It wasn't a true part of the swamp but a slow, meandering, mud-brown creek, perhaps twenty feet across, if that. There was a hitching-post nearby, with a similar one at the far bank. Also by the far bank was a warped and aged craft which not even the charitable could have called a boat. It was built along the lines of an over-sized coffin, with a squared-off end where the bows should have been. The ferry – probably the most kindly name for it – was attached to the two hitching-posts by an endless pulley.

The two dog-handlers hauled the boat across, got into it with understandable caution, and were joined by their dogs, who kept on displaying considerable signs of animation, an animation which rapidly diminished then vanished shortly after they had landed on the far bank. After making a few fruitless circles, they lay down dejectedly on the ground.

'Well, ain't that a shame,' a voice said. 'Trail gone cold, I guess.'

The four men on the near bank turned to look at the source of the voice. He was a bizarre character, wearing a new panama hat with a tartan band, gleaming thigh-length leather boots (presumably as a protection against snakebites) and clothes discarded by a scarecrow. 'You folks chasin' someone?'

'We're looking for someone,' McGarrity said cautiously.

'Lawmen, yes?'

'Chief of Police McGarrity.'

'Honoured, I'm sure. Well, Chief, you're wasting your time. Hot trail here, cold on the other side. So, the party you're looking for got off half-way across.'

'You saw them?' McGarrity asked suspiciously.

'Hah! More than one, eh? No, sir. Just happened by right now. But if I was on the run from the law that's what I'd do because it's been done hundreds of times. You can get out midway, walk half a mile, even a mile, up-stream or down-stream. Dozens of little rivulets come into this creek. You could turn up any of those, go a mile into the swamp without setting foot on dry land Wouldn't find them this side of Christmas, Chief'

'How deep is the creek?'

'Fifteen inches. If that'

'Then why the boat? I mean, with those boots you could walk across without getting your feet wet?'

The stranger looked almost shocked. 'No siree. Takes me an hour every morning to polish up them critters.' It was assumed that he was referring to his boots. 'Besides, they're the water-moccasins.' He seemed to have a rooted aversion to snakes. 'The boat? Come the rains, the creek's up to here.' He touched his chest

McGarrity called the dog-handlers to return. Mitchell said to the stranger: 'Any place in the swamps where a helicopter could land?'

'Sure. More firm land out there than there is swamp-land. Never seen any helicopters, though Yes, lots of clearings.'

The dog-handlers and dogs disembarked. Leaving the stranger to flick some invisible dust off his boots, they made their way back to the estate wagon. Mitchell said· 'A moment. I've just had a thought.' He opened up the two plastic bags containing the dressing-gowns and presented them to the dogs again. He then walked back up the rutted lane, past the two cars and van, beckoning the dog-handlers to follow him, which they did, almost having to drag the reluctant dogs behind them

After about twenty yards the reluctance vanished. The dogs yelped and strained at their leashes For another twenty yards they towed their handlers along behind them, then abruptly stopped and circled a few times before sitting down dispiritedly Mitchell crouched and examined the surface of the lane The others caught up with him.

McGarrity said: 'What gives, then?'

'This.' Mitchell pointed to the ground. 'There was another vehicle here. You can see where its back wheels spun when it started to reverse. The kidnappers guessed we'd be using tracker dogs – it wasn't all that hard a guess. So they carried the girls twenty yards or so, to break the scent, before setting them down again.'

'Right smart of you, Mr Mitchell, right smart.' McGarrity didn't look as pleased as his words made out. 'So the birds have flown, eh? And now we haven't the faintest idea what the getaway vehicle looks like.'

Roomer said: 'Somebody's flown, that's for sure. But maybe only one or two. Maybe they've gone to borrow a helicopter.'

'A helicopter?' The waters didn't have to be very deep for Chief McGarrity to start floundering.

With a trace of weary impatience Mitchell said: 'It could be a double bluff. Maybe they reversed the procedure and took the girls back to the station wagon again. Maybe they are still in the swamp, waiting for a helicopter to come and pick them up. You heard the old boy back there – he said there were plenty of places in the swamp where a helicopter could touch down.'

McGarrity nodded sagely and appeared to ponder the matter deeply. The time had come, he felt, for him to make a positive contribution. 'The swamp's out. Hopeless. So I'll have to concentrate on the helicopter angle.'

Mitchell said: 'How do you propose to do that?'

'Just you leave that to me.'

Roomer said· 'That's hardly fair, Mr McGarrity. We've given you our complete confidence. Don't you think we're entitled to some in return?'

'Well, now.' McGarrity appeared to ruminate, although he was secretly pleased to be asked the question, as Roomer had known he would be. 'If the chopper doesn't get in there, it can't very well lift them out, can it?'

'That's a fact,' Roomer said solemnly.

'So I station marksmen round this side of the swamp. It's no great deal to bring down a low-flying chopper.'

Mitchell said: 'I wouldn't do that if I were you.'

'No indeed.' Roomer shook his head. 'The law frowns on murder.'

'Murder?' McGarrity stared at them 'Who's talking of murder?'

'We are,' Mitchell said. 'Rifle or machine-gun fire might well kill someone inside the helicopter If it brings down the helicopter they'd all probably die. Maybe there are criminals aboard, but they're entitled to a fair trial before execution. And has it occurred to you that the pilot will almost certainly be an innocent party with a pistol pointed at his head?' McGarrity, clearly, had not thought of that. 'Not going to make us very popular, is it?'

McGarrity winced. Even the very thought of unpopularity and the forthcoming election made him feel pale inside.

'So what the devil do we do?'

Roomer was frank. 'I'll be damned if I know. You can post observers. You can even have a grounded helicopter standing by to chase the other one when it takes off. If, that's to say, it ever comes in the first place. We're only guessing.'

'No more we can do here,' Mitchell said. 'We've already missed too many appointments today. We'll be in touch.

Back on the highway Roomer said: 'How do you think he'd do as a dog-catcher?'

'Place would be overrun by stray dogs in a few months

How much faith do you have in this idea that they might use a helicopter?'

'Quite a lot. If they just wanted to change cars they wouldn't have gone through this elaborate rigmarole. They could have parked their station wagon out of sight almost any place. By apparently going into hiding in the swamp they hoped to give the impression that they were preparing to hole up in there for quite some time to come. They hadn't figured on our backing - your back-tracking - up the lane.'

'We're pretty sure that their destination is the *Seawitch*. We're pretty sure they'll use a helicopter. Which helicopter and pilot would you use?'

'Lord Worth's. Not only are his pilots almost certainly the only ones who know the exact co-ordinates of the *Seawitch*, but the very distinctly marked Worth Hudson helicopters are the only ones that could approach the *Seawitch* without raising suspicion.' Roomer reached for the phone, fiddled with the waveband and raised Lord Worth's house. 'Jim?'

'At my post, Mr Roomer.'

'We're coming back there. Look for Lord Worth's address book. Probably right by you in your radio room Make us a list of the names and addresses of his helicopter pilots. Is the gate-keeper at the heliport on the radio-phone, too?'

'Yes.'

'Get that for us too, please.'

'Will do.'

He said to Mitchell: 'Still think we shouldn't warn Larsen about our suspicions?'

'That's for sure.' Mitchell was very definite. 'The *Seawitch* is Larsen's baby, and the kind of reception he'd prepare might all too easily be over-enthusiastic. Or would you care for the job of explaining to Lord Worth how come his daughters got caught in the cross-fire?'

'I would not.' Roomer spoke with some feeling.

'Or even explaining to yourself how Melinda got shot through the lung?'

Roomer ignored him. 'What if we're wrong in our guesses about his lordship's pilots?'

'Then turn the whole thing over to that ace detective, McGarrity.'

'So we'd better be right.'

They were right. They were also too late.

John Campbell was both an avid fisherman and an avid reader. He had long since mastered the techniques of indulging his two pleasures simultaneously. A creek, fairly popular with fish, ran within twenty feet of his back porch. Campbell was sitting on a canvas chair, parasol over his head, alternating every page with a fresh cast of his line, when Durand and one of his men, stocking-masked and holding guns in their hands, came into his line of vision. Campbell rose to his feet, book still in hand.

'Who are you and what do you want?'

'You. You're Campbell, aren't you?'

'What if I am?'

'Like you to do a little job for us.'

'What job?'

'Fly a helicopter for us.'

'I'll be damned if I do!'

'So you *are* Campbell. Come along.'

Following the gesturing of their guns Campbell moved between the two men. He was within one foot of Durand's gun hand when he chopped the side of his hand on the wrist that held the gun. Durand grunted in pain, the gun fell to the ground and a second later the two men were locked together, wrestling, kicking and punching with a fine disregard for the rules of sport, altering position so

126

frequently that Durand's henchman, gun barrel now in his hand – the last thing he wanted to do was to shoot Campbell - at first found no opportunity to intervene But the opportunity came very soon. The unsportsmanlike but effective use of Campbell's right knee doubled Durand over in gasping agony, but enough instinct was left him to seize Campbell's shirt as he fell over backwards. This was Campbell's downfall in more ways than one, for the back of his head simply cried out for the attentions of a gun-butt

The man who had felled Campbell pulled Campbell clear, allowing Durand to climb painfully to his feet, although still bent over at an angle of 45 degrees. He pulled off his stocking mask as if to try to gain access to more air. Durand, surprisingly, was Latin American He had a pale, coffee-coloured face, thick black curling hair and a pencil-line moustache and might even have proved to be handsome when the twisted lines of agony ceased to contort his face. He straightened inch by inch and finally obtained a modicum of breath, enough, at least, to allow him to announce what he would like to do with Campbell.

'Have to be some other time, Mr Durand He can't very well fly a chopper from a hospital bed '

Durand painfully acknowledged the truth of this 'I hope *you* didn't hit him too hard '

'Just a tap.'

'Tie him, tape him and blindfold him.' Durand was now about twenty degrees off the vertical. His helpmate left for the car and returned in moments with cord, tape and blindfold. Three minutes later they were on their way, with a rug-covered and still unconscious Campbell on the floor at the back. Resting comfortably on the rug were Durand's feet - he still didn't feel quite up to driving. Both men had their masks off now – even in the free

wheeling state of Florida men with stocking masks in cars
were apt to draw just a little more than passing attention

Mitchell glanced briefly at the list of names and addresses
Robertson had given them. 'Fine. But what are those
ticks opposite five of the names?'

Robertson sounded apologetic. 'I hope you don't
mind – I don't want to seem interfering – but I took the
liberty of phoning those gentlemen to see if they would be
at home when you called. I assumed you'd be calling
because you asked for the addresses.'

Mitchell looked at Roomer. 'Why the hell didn't you
think of that?'

Roomer bestowed a cold glance on him and said to
Robertson, 'Maybe I should have you as a partner.
What did you find out?'

'One pilot is standing by at the airport. Four of the
others are at home. The one whose name I haven't ticked
Mr John Campbell - isn't home. I asked one of the
other pilots about this, and he seemed a bit surprised.
Said that Mr Campbell usually spends his afternoons
fishing outside the back of his house. He's a bachelor and
lives in a pretty isolated place.'

'It figures,' Roomer said. 'A bachelor in isolation. The
kidnappers seem to have an excellent intelligence system.
The fact that he doesn't answer the phone may mean
nothing – he could have gone for a walk, shopping,
visiting friends. On the other hand - '

'Yes. Especially on the other hand.' Mitchell turned to
leave, then said to Robertson: 'Does the gate-keeper have a
listed phone number as well as the radio-phone?'

I've typed it on that list.'

'Maybe we should both have you as a partner '

Mitchell and Roomer stood on Campbell's back lawn

and surveyed the scene unemotionally The canvas chair, on its side, had a broken leg. The parasol was at full length on the grass, straddling an upturned book. The fishing rod was in the water up to its handle, and would have floated away had not the reel snagged on a shrub root. Roomer retrieved the rod while Mitchell hurried through the back doorway – the back door was wide open, as was the front. He dialled a phone number, which answered on the first ring.

'Lord Worth's heliport. Gorrie here.'

'My name's Mitchell. You have a police guard?'

'Mr Mitchell? You Lord Worth's friend?'

'Yes.'

'Sergeant Roper is here.'

'That all? Let me speak to him.' There was hardly a pause before Roper came on the phone.

'Mike? Nice to hear from you again.'

'Listen, Sergeant, this is urgent. I'm speaking from the house of John Campbell, one of Lord Worth's pilots. He has been forcibly abducted, almost certainly by some of the kidnappers of Lord Worth's daughters. I have every reason to believe – no time for explanations now – that they are heading in your direction with the intention of hijacking one of Lord Worth's helicopters and forcing Campbell to fly it. There'll be two of them at least, maybe three, armed and dangerous. I suggest you call up reinforcements immediately. If we get them we'll break them – at least Roomer and I will, you can't, you're a law officer and your hands are tied – and we'll find where the girls are and get them back.'

'Reinforcements coming up. Then I'll look the other way.'

Mitchell hung up. Roomer was by his side. Roomer said: 'You prepared to resort to torture to get the information you want?'

Mitchell looked at him bleakly 'I look forward to it Don't you?'

'No. But I'll go along with you.'

Once again Mitchell and Roomer had guessed correctly. And once again they were too late.

Mitchell had driven to Lord Worth's heliport with a minimum regard for traffic and speed regulations, and now, having arrived there, realized bitterly that his haste had been wholly unnecessary.

Five men greeted their arrival, although it was hardly a cheerful meeting: Gorrie, the gateman, and four policemen. Gorrie and Sergeant Roper were tenderly massaging their wrists. Mitchell looked at Roper.

'Don't tell me.' Mitchell sounded weary. 'They jumped you before the reinforcements were to hand.'

'Yes.' Roper's face was dark with anger. 'I know it sounds like the old lame excuse, but we never had a chance. This car comes along and stops outside the gatehouse, just here. The driver – he was alone in the car – seemed to be having a fit of sneezes and was holding a big wad of Kleenex to his face.'

Roomer said: 'So you wouldn't recognize him again?'

'Exactly. Well, we were watching this character when a voice behind us – the back window was open – told us to freeze. I didn't even have my hand on my gun. We froze. Then he told me to drop my gun. Well, this guy was no more than five feet away and I had my back to him. I dropped my gun. Dead heroes are no good to anyone Then he told us to turn round. He was wearing a stocking mask. Then the driver came in and tied our wrists behind our backs. When we turned round he was wearing a stocking mask too.'

'Then they tied your feet and tied you together so that

you wouldn't have any funny ideas about using a tele-phone?'

'That's how it was. But they weren't worried about the phones. They smashed them both before they took off.'

'They took off immediately?'

Gorrie said: 'No. Five minutes later. The pilots always radio-file a flight plan before take-off. I suppose the kidnappers forced Campbell to do the same. To make it look kosher.'

Mitchell shrugged his indifference. 'Means nothing. You can file a flight plan to any place. Doesn't mean you have to keep it. How about fuel – for the helicopters, I mean?'

'Fuel's always kept topped up. My job. Lord Worth's orders '

'What direction did the kidnappers go?'

'That-away.' Gorrie indicated with an outstretched arm.

'Well, the birds have flown. Might as well be on our way.'

'Just like that?' Roper registered surprise.

'What do you expect me to do that the police can't?'

'Well, for starters, we could call in the air force.'

'Why?'

'They could force it down.'

Mitchell sighed. 'There's a great deal of rubbish talked about forcing planes down. What if they refuse to be forced down?'

'Then shoot it down.'

'With Lord Worth's daughters aboard? Lord Worth wouldn't be very pleased. Neither would you. Think of all the cops that would be out of a job.'

'Lord Worth's daughters!'

'It's all this routine police work,' Roomer said. 'Atrophies the brain. Who the hell do you think that helicopter has gone to pick up?'

Once clear of the heliport Roomer extended an arm. ' "That-away" the man said "That-away" is north-west. The Wyanee swamp.'

'Even if they'd taken off to the south-east they'd still have finished up in Wyanee.' Mitchell pulled up by a public booth 'How are you with McGarrity's voice?' Roomer was an accomplished mimic

'It's not the voice that worries me It's the thought processes. I'll give it a try' He didn't say what he was going to try because he didn't have to He left for the booth and was back inside two minutes

'Campbell filed a flight plan for the *Seawitch*

'Any questions asked?'

'Not really Told them that some fool had made a mistake. Anyone who knows McGarrity would know the identity of the fool that made the mistake'

Mitchell switched on the engine then switched off as the phone rang. Mitchell lifted the receiver

'Jim here Tried to ring you a couple of times, fifteen minutes ago, five minutes ago'

'Figures. Out of the car both times More bad news?'

'Not unless you consider Lord Worth bad news Touch down in fifteen minutes'

'We've time'

'Says he's coming up to the house.'

'Sent for the Rolls?'

'No. Probably wants to talk private. And it looks as if he's planning to stay away some time Ordered a bag packed for a week.'

'Seven white suits.' Mitchell hung up

Roomer said: 'Looks as if we're going to have to do some bag-packing ourselves.' Mitchell nodded and

132

switched on again.

Lord Worth was looking his old self when he settled in the back seat of their car. Not quite radiating his old bonhomie, to be sure, but calm and lucid and, to all appearances, relaxed. He told of his success in Washington, for which he was duly and politely congratulated. Roomer then told him in detail what had happened in his absence · this time the absence of congratulations was marked.

'You've notified Commander Larsen of your sus picions, of course ?'

'Not suspicions,' Mitchell said. 'Certainties And there's no "of course" and no, we didn't notify him. I'm primarily responsible for that.'

'Taking the law into your own hands, eh? Mind telling me why ?'

'You're the person who knows Larsen best. You know how possessive he is about the *Seawitch*. You yourself have told us about his anger and violence. Do you think a man like that, duly forewarned, wouldn't have a very warm reception waiting for the kidnappers? Stray bullets, ricocheting bullets, are no respecters of persons, Lord Worth. You want a daughter crippled for life? We prefer that the kidnappers establish a bloodless beach-head.'

'Well, all right.' The words came grudgingly. 'But from now on keep me fully informed of your intentions and decisions.' Lord Worth, Roomer noted with sardonic amusement, had no intention of dispensing with their unpaid services 'But no more taking the law into your own hands, do you hear?'

Mitchell stopped car and engine. Roomer's amusement changed to apprehension. Mitchell twisted in his seat and looked at Lord Worth in cool speculation.

'You're a fine one to talk.'

'What do you mean, sir ?' There were fifteen generations

of Highland aristocracy in the glacial voice.

Mitchell remained unmoved. 'For taking the law into your own hands by breaking into and robbing that armoury last night. If Roomer and I were decent citizens and law-abiding detectives, we'd have had you behind bars last night. Not even a billionaire can get off with that sort of thing, especially when it involves the assault and locking up of the armoury guards. John and I were there.' Mitchell was not above a little prevarication when the need arose.

'*You* were there?' Most rarely for him, Lord Worth was at a loss for words. He recovered quickly. 'But *I* wasn't there.'

'We know that. We also know you sanctioned the break-in. Ordered it, rather.'

'Balderdash. And if you actually witnessed this, why did you not stop it?'

'John and I take our chances. But not against nine men armed with nine machine-guns.'

This gave Lord Worth to pause. They had their figures and facts right. Clearly they had been there. He said: 'Supposing any of this rigmarole were true, how in God's name do you tie me up with this?'

'Now you're being a fool. We were also at your heliport. We saw the truck arrive. We saw nine men unload a fairly massive quantity of more than fairly lethal weaponry into one helicopter. Then a man drove the truck away - an army truck, of course – back to the armoury from where it had been stolen. The other eight men boarded another helicopter. Then a mini-bus arrived, carrying twelve heavily-armed thugs, who joined the other eight. John and I recognized no fewer than five of them   two of them we've personally put behind bars.' Roomer looked at him admiringly, but Mitchell wasn't looking at him, he was looking at Lord Worth, and both voice and tone were bereft of any form of encouragement. 'It came as a shock to both of us to find that Lord Worth was consorting with common criminals. Your brow is very damp, Lord Worth. Why is it very damp?'

Lord Worth **didn't** enlighten them as to the reason why his brow was damp.

'And then, of course, you came along in the Rolls One of the very best sequences we got on our infra-red ciné camera last night.' Roomer choked, but the peculiar coughing sound had no effect on Lord Worth, who was now perspiring freely. That Lord Worth believed Mitchell, Roomer did not for a moment doubt: everything that Mitchell had said, even the slight embellishments, Lord Worth knew or believed to be true, so he had no reason to doubt the truth of the ciné camera fiction.

'We actually debated phoning the nearest army HQ and have them send along some armoured cars and a trailered tank. Even your murderous thugs would have stood no chance. We thought of going down the road, blocking the Rolls and holding you until the army arrived – it was perfectly obvious that the helicopters had no intention of leaving until you turned up. Once captured, God knows how many of them – especially those who had already served prison terms – would have jumped at the chance of turning State's evidence and incriminating you. It's quite true, you know – there *is* no honour among thieves.' If Lord Worth had any objection to being categorized as a thief it didn't register in his face. 'But after the standard bit of soul-searching we decided against it.'

'Why, in God's name?'

'So you admit it.' Mitchell sighed. 'Why couldn't you do that at the beginning and save me all this trouble?'

'Why?' Lord Worth repeated his question.

It was Roomer who answered. 'Partly because even

though you're a confessed law-breaker, we still have a regard for you. But it's chiefly because we didn't want to see your daughters confronted with the unedifying spectacle of seeing their father behind bars. In hindsight, of course, we're extremely glad we didn't. In comparison with the kidnapping of your daughters, your own ventures outside the law fade into something that is comparatively a peccadillo.'

Mitchell started the motor again and said: 'It is understood that there will be no more such peccadilloes again. It is also understood that there will be no more silly talk as to whether we take the law into our own hands or not.'

Lord Worth lay back in his study armchair. His second brandy tasted just as good as his first – it seemed to be his day for brandies. He hadn't spoken a word for the rest of the trip which, fortunately, had been mercifully short, for Lord Worth had felt urgently in need of restoratives. Not for the first time he found himself silently blessing his kidnapped daughters.

He cleared his throat and said: 'I assume you are still willing to come out to the rig with me?'

Mitchell contemplated his glass. 'We never expressed our intentions one way or another about that. But I suppose someone has to look after you and your daughters.'

Lord Worth frowned. There had, he felt, been more than a subtle change in their relationship. Perhaps the establishment of an employer-employee status would help redress the balance. He said: 'I feel it's time we put your co-operation on a business-like footing. I propose to retain you in your professional capacities as investigators, in other words to become your client. I shall not quibble at your demanded fees.' He had no sooner finished than he realized that he had made a mistake.

Roomer's voice was coldly unenthusiastic. 'Money

doesn't buy everything, Lord Worth. Particularly, it doesn't buy us. What you are proposing is that you establish a moral ascendancy on the basis of the man who pays the piper calls the tune. We have no intention of being shackled, of having our freedom of action curtailed. And as to the question of fees and your "sky's-the-limit" inference, the hell with your fees. How often do you have to be told that we don't barter money for your daughters' lives?'

'Hear, hear,' Mitchell said 'Couldn't have put it better myself.'

Lord Worth didn't even bother frowning. The change in relationship, he reflected sadly, had been even greater than he had realized. 'As you will. One assumes that you will be suitably disguised?'

Mitchell said: 'Why?'

Lord Worth was impatient. 'You said you saw some ex-convicts boarding the helicopter. People you recognized. They'll surely recognize you?'

'We never saw any of them before in our lives.'

Lord Worth was properly shocked. 'But you told me – '

'You told us big black lies. What's a little white lie? Let's go aboard as – say – your technological advisers. Geologists, seismologists – it's all the same to us, we know nothing about geology or seismology. All we need are a couple of well-cut business suits, panamas, horn-rimmed glasses with plain lenses – for the studious look – and brief-cases.' He paused. 'And we'll also need a doctor, with full medical kit and a large supply of bandages.'

'A doctor?'

'For extracting bullets, sewing up gunshot wounds. Or are you so naive as to believe that there will be no shot fired in anger aboard the *Seawitch*?'

'I abhor violence.'

'Sure. That's why you sent twenty heavily-armed thugs

out to the *Seawitch* during the night? Fine, so you abhor violence. Others welcome it. Can you lay hands on such a doctor?'

'Dozens of them. The average doctor hereabouts rates his scanning of X-rays a very poor second to the scanning of his bank balances. I know the man. Greenshaw. After seven years in Vietnam, he should fit your bill.'

Roomer said: 'And ask him to bring along two spare white lab-coats.'

'Why?' Mitchell said.

'Want to look scientific, don't you?

Lord Worth picked up the phone, made the arrangements, replaced the receiver and said: 'You must excuse me. I have some private calls to make from the radio room.' Lord Worth's sole reason for returning to his house was to contact his inside man, Corral, and have him, without incriminating himself, inform Benson, who had hosted the Lake Tahoe meeting, that the Government intended to blast out of the water any foreign naval ships that approached the *Seawitch*. An exaggeration but, Lord Worth thought, a pardonable one. Despite the Secretary's promise, Lord Worth placed more faith in his direct approach.

Mitchell said: 'Which one of us do you want to go with you?'

'What do you mean? "Private", I said.' His face darkened in anger. 'Am I to be ordered around in my own house, supervised as if I'm an irresponsible child?'

'You behaved responsibly last night? Look, Lord Worth, if you don't want either of us around, then it's obvious you want to say something that you don't want us to hear.' Mitchell gave him a speculative look. 'I don't like that. You're either up to something we'd disapprove of, something shady if you like, or it's a vote of no confidence in us.'

'It's a personal and highly important business call I don't see why you should be privy to my business affairs.'

Roomer said: 'I agree. But it so happens that we don't think that it is a business call, that business would be the last thing in your mind at such a time.' Both Mitchell and Roomer stood up. 'Give our regards to the girls – if you ever find them.'

'Blackmail! Damned blackmail!' Lord Worth rapidly weighed the importance of his call to Corral compared to the importance of having Mitchell and Roomer around. It took all of two seconds to make up his mind, and Corral was clear out of sight at the winning post. He was sure that the two men were bluffing, but there was no way he could call their bluff, for that was the one sure way of provoking a genuine walk-out.

Lord Worth put on his stony face. 'I suppose I have no option other than to accede to your threats. I suggest you go and pack your bags and I'll pick you up in the Rolls.'

Mitchell said: 'Packing will take minutes. I feel it would be much more polite if we were to wait here until you're ready.'

Lord Worth glared at him. 'You think I'd head for a telephone the moment your backs are turned?'

Mitchell smiled. 'Isn't it odd that the same thought should occur to the three of us at the same instant?'

chapter
7

Commander Larsen and Scoffield observed the approach of the Worth Hudson helicopter with surprise but without undue concern. Lord Worth customarily gave advance warning of his arrival but could occasionally be forgetful on this point. In any event it was his helicopter, and this should be about his expected time of arrival. They sauntered across the platform and arrived at the north-east helipad just as the helicopter touched down.

Surprisingly, no one emerged immediately from the machine. Larsen and Scoffield looked at each other in some perplexity, a perplexity that was considerably deepened when the disembarkation door slid back and Durand appeared in the doorway with a machine-pistol cradled in his hands. Just behind him stood a similarly equipped henchman. From their shadowed position it was impossible for them to be observed by any of the rig duty crew.

Durand said: 'Larsen and Scoffield? If you are carrying weapons please don't be so foolish as to try to use them.' The boarding steps swung down. 'Come and join us.'

The two men had no option. Once aboard, without taking his eyes off them, Durand said: 'Kowenski, Rindler – see if they are armed.'

Both Larsen and Scoffield carried automatics but seemed quite indifferent to being deprived of them: their attention was directed exclusively to the presence of Lord Worth's daughters.

Marina smiled, albeit a trifle wanly. 'We could have met under happier circumstances, Commander.'

Larsen nodded. 'Your kidnappers. This can carry a death sentence.' He looked at Campbell. 'Why did you fly those criminals out here?'

'Because I come over all cowardly when I have a pistol barrel screwed into the back of my neck all the way from take-off to touch-down.' Campbell spoke with a certain justifiable bitterness.

Larsen looked at Melinda. 'Have you been maltreated in any fashion?'

'No.'

'And they won't be,' Durand said. 'Unless, of course, you refuse to do as we tell you.'

'What does that mean?'

'You close down the Christmas tree. This meant closing off all the oil supplies from the ocean floor.

'I'll be damned if I do.' Larsen's dark piratical face was suffused with fury. Here, Durand realized, was a man who, even without arms, could be highly dangerous. He glanced briefly at Rindler, who struck Larsen on the back of the neck with the butt of his machine-pistol, a shrewdly calculated blow designed to daze but not knock out. When Larsen's head had cleared he found that he had bracelets around both wrists and ankles. His attention then focused on a pair of gleaming stainless steel medical cutters of the type much favoured by the surgical fraternity for snipping through ribs. The handles were in Durand's firm grip: the unpleasant operating end was closed lightly round the little finger of Melinda's right hand.

Durand said: 'Lord Worth isn't going to like you too much for this, Larsen.'

Larsen, apparently, was of the same opinion 'Take

those damned pliers away and my bracelets off. I'll close
down your damned Christmas tree '

'And I'll come with you just to see that you really do
turn off this Christmas tree. Not that I would recognize
one of those things if I saw it, but I do know that there are
such things as flow gauges. I shall carry a walkie-talkie
with me Aaron here has another. I shall keep in constant
contact with him. If anything should happen to me - '
Durand looked consideringly at the medical cutters, then
handed them to Heffer, the fifth man in his team He told
Campbell to put his arms behind his seat-back and
handcuffed his wrists

'Don't miss much, do you ?' Larsen's voice was sour

'You know how it is So many villains around these days.
Come on '

The two men walked across the platform in the direction
of the drilling rig. After only a few paces Durand stopped
and looked around him admiringly

'Well, well, now. Dual-purpose anti-aircraft guns. Piles
of depth-charges. One would almost think that you were
prepared to withstand a siege. Dear me, dear me. Federal
offence, you know. Lord Worth, even with the millions
he can pay for lawyers, can't fail to spend at least ten
years in penitentiary for this '

'What *are* you talking about ?'

'Hardly standard equipment aboard an oil rig. I'll
wager it wasn't here twenty-four hours ago. I'll wager it
was inside the Mississippi naval armoury that was broken
into last night The Government takes a very dim view of
people who steal its military equipment. And, of course,
you must have specialists aboard who are skilled in
handling such equipment, and that's hardly part of the
basic training of oil rig crews. I wonder if those crews are
also carrying special equipment – such, for instance, as
was stolen from a Florida armoury last night. I mean, two

142

unrelated armoury break-ins in the same night is just too much of a coincidence. Twenty years in prison with no possibility of remission for you too, as the person chiefly responsible for aiding and abetting. And people call *us* criminals!'

Larsen had a few choice observations to make in return, none of which would have received the approval of even the most tolerant board of censors.

The Christmas tree was duly neutralized. The pressure gauges registered zero. Durand turned his attention to the *Roamer*, carrying out its short and wearisome patrol between the rig and the huge floating oil tank. 'What's our friend up to?'

'Even a land-lubber like you should be able to guess. He's patrolling the pipe-line.'

'What on earth for? You could replace a cut line in a day. What would that achieve? It's crazy.'

'You have to use crazy methods to deal with crazy people. From all accounts Lord Worth's enemies should be locked up for their own good. For everybody's good.'

'Worth's band of cut-throats aboard this rig? Who's their leader?'

'Giuseppe Palermo.'

'That mobster! So the noble lord, apart from indulging in grand larceny, is a known associate of criminals and convicted felons.'

'You know him, then?'

'Yes.' Durand saw no point in elaborating upon the fact that he and Palermo had spent two prison terms together. 'I want to talk to him.'

The talk was brief and one-sided. Durand said: 'We've got Lord Worth's daughters prisoner. You're Lord Worth's men, so we know that no harm will come to them from you. We're bringing them towards the living quarters here but they will not mingle with you – we don't want you to take our two aces away from us. You will remain inside your quarters. If you don't you're likely to hear quite a lot of screaming and see bits and pieces of fingers or ears being dropped through your windows. I hope you believe me.'

Palermo believed him. Palermo had a reputation for ruthlessness that matched Durand's, but it couldn't begin to match Durand's unholy joy in sadism. Durand was perfectly capable of not only doing what he threatened but of deriving immense satisfaction in so doing.

Palermo returned to his Oriental quarters. Durand called up Rindler on the walkie-talkie and told them all to come across, including Campbell, the pilot: Campbell was tough and resourceful and it was just possible that, by standing up, he could slip his manacled arms over the back of his seat, step through them and take off. Whether he would have enough fuel for the return flight would be a problem for him, even though he would almost certainly head, not for Florida, but for the nearest spot on the mainland, which would be due south of New Orleans.

As the prisoners and guards disembarked from the helicopter Durand said: 'Accommodation?'

'Plenty. There are spare rooms in the Oriental quarters. There's Lord Worth's private suite.'

'Lock-ups?'

'What do you mean? This isn't a prison.'

'Store-rooms? Ones that can be locked from the outside.'

'Yes.'

Durand looked at Larsen consideringly. 'You're being extremely co-operative, Larsen. Your reputation says otherwise.'

'Two minutes' walk around and you could confirm all I'm saying for yourself.'

'You'd like to kill me, wouldn't you, Larsen?'

'When the time is ripe, yes. But it's not yet.'

'Even so.' Durand produced a pistol. 'Stay about ten feet away. You might be tempted to attack me and tell our men that you'll tear me limb from limb unless they release the girls. A tempting thought, no?'

Larsen looked at him yearningly and said nothing.

The girls, the pilots and their four escorts arrived. Durand said: 'Well, now, we must find some suitable overnight accommodation for you.' He led the way to the first of several store-houses and opened the door to reveal a room packed roof-high with tinned foods. He bundled Campbell inside, locked the door and pocketed the key. The next store-house contained coils of rope, a powerful smell of crude oil and an active, scuttling population of those indestructible creatures, cockroaches. Durand said to the two girls: 'Inside.'

The girls took one shuddering look then turned away Marina said· 'We will not go inside that disgusting place.'

Kowenski said in a gently-chiding voice which accorded ill with the Colt he held in his hand: 'Don't you know what this is?' Rindler had a similar weapon trained on Melinda.

Both girls glanced briefly at each other and then, in what was obviously a prepared and rehearsed movement, walked towards the men with the guns, seized the barrels with their right hands and hooked their right thumbs behind the trigger forefingers, pulling the guns hard against themselves.

Marina said: 'I can squeeze my thumb far faster than you can jerk that gun away. Want to try?'

'Jesus Christ!' Durand was badly shaken. He had run up against most situations in his life, but this one lay far beyond his most remote conception. 'You trying to commit suicide?'

Melinda said: 'Precisely.' Her eyes never left Rindler's.

145

'You're lower than those horrible cockroaches in there. You are vermin who are trying to destroy our father. With us dead you won't have a single card left to play.'

'You're crazy! Simple plain crazy!'

'That's as may be,' Marina said. 'But for crazy people our logic is pretty good. With nothing to shackle his hands you can imagine how our father will react – especially as he will believe, as everybody will believe, that you murdered us. He won't have recourse to the law, of course – you simply have no idea what power a few billion dollars can bring to bear. He'll destroy you and all your criminal associates to the last man.' She looked at Kowenski with contempt. 'Why don't you press the trigger? No? Then drop your gun.' Kowenski dropped his gun and Rindler did the same.

Melinda said: 'My sister and I are taking a walk. We will return when you have quarters prepared fitting for Lord Worth's daughters.'

Durand's face had definitely lost colour and his voice was hoarse and not quite steady as he tried to regain a measure of authority. 'Have your walk if you must. Heffer, go with them. Any trouble, shoot them in the legs.'

Marina stooped, picked up Kowenski's Colt, walked up to Heffer and rammed the muzzle into his left eye. Heffer howled in agony. Marina said: 'Fair deals. You shoot me through the leg – now, I mean - and I'll blow your brains out.'

'God's sake!' Durand's voice was almost imploring. He was just one step removed from wringing his hands. 'Somebody's got to go with you. If you're out there on your own and in no danger, Palermo's men will cut us to pieces.'

'What a perfectly splendid idea.' Marina withdrew the pistol from an already bruising eye, and looked in distaste at Heffer, a rodent-faced creature of indeterminate age

146

and nationality. 'We see your point. But this – this animal is not to approach within ten yards of us at any time That is understood ?'

'Yes, yes, of course.' If they asked him for the moon Durand would have levitated himself and got it for them. Having overwhelmingly displayed what it was to have sixteen generations of Highland aristocratic ancestry, the two girls walked away towards one of the triangular perimeters. It was fully twenty yards before they both began, at the same instant, to tremble violently. Once started, they could not control the trembling and they prayed that the following Heffer could not notice it.

Marina whispered shakily: 'Would you do that again?'

'Never, never, never. I'd rather die.'

'I think we came pretty close to it. Do you think that Michael and John would be shaking like us after an experience like that?'

'No. If there's any truth in half the hints Daddy lets drop, they'd already be planning what to do next. And Durand and his obnoxious friends wouldn't be shaking either. Dead men don't shake very much.'

Marina's trembling turned into a genuine shiver 'I only wish to God they were here right now.'

They stopped ten feet short of the platform perimeter. Neither girl had a head for heights. They turned and looked north-eastwards as the distant and muted roar of an aero-engine came to their ears.

Durand and Larsen heard it at the same time. They could see nothing because dusk had already fallen, but neither man had any doubts as to the identity of the approaching helicopter and its occupants. With some satisfaction Durand said: 'Company. This has to be Lord Worth. Where will they land?'

'The south-east helipad.'

Durand glanced across the platform to where the two

girls were standing with Heffer, gun carried loosely in his right hand, less than the regulation ten yards away Satisfied, Durand picked up his machine-pistol and said: 'Let's go and welcome his lordship aboard. Aaron, come with us.'

Larsen said: 'You'd better hope that Lord Worth proves a bit more tractable than his daughters.'

'What do you mean?'

Larsen smiled in sardonic satisfaction. 'You really did catch a couple of tigresses by their tails, didn't you?'

Durand scowled and walked away, followed by Larsen and Aaron, the latter armed similarly to Durand. They reached the south-east helipad just as the Worth Hudson helicopter touched down. Lord Worth himself was the first out. He stood at the foot of the steps and stared in disbelief at the armed men. He said to Larsen: 'What in God's name goes on here?'

Durand said: 'Welcome aboard the *Seawitch*, Lord Worth. You may regard me as your host and yourself as a guest – an honoured guest, of course. There has been a slight change of ownership.'

'I'm afraid that this man here – his name is Durand and one must assume that he is one of Cronkite's lieutenants – '

'Cronkite!' Durand was jarred. 'What do you know about Cronkite?'

'I can hardly congratulate him on his choice of lieutenants.' When Lord Worth poured on his icy contempt he used a king-sized can. 'Do you think we are such fools as not to know who your paymaster is? Not that Mr Cronkite has long to live. Nor you, either, for that matter.' Durand stirred uneasily; Lord Worth sounded far too much like his daughters for his peace of mind. Lord Worth directed his attention to Larsen. 'One assumes that this ruffian arrived with accomplices. How many?'

'Four '

Four! But with Palermo and his men you have over twenty! How is it possible – '

Durand was back on balance. When he spoke it was with a slight if pardonable smugness. 'We have something that Larsen hasn't. We have your daughters.'

What was apparently pure shock rendered Lord Worth temporarily speechless, then in a hoarse voice he said: 'Great God Almighty! My daughters!' Lord Worth could have had his Oscar just for the asking. 'You – *you* are the kidnapper?'

'Fortunes of war, sir.' It said much for Lord Worth's aristocratic magnetism that even the most villainous eventually addressed him in respectful tones. 'Now, if we could see the rest of the passengers.'

Mitchell and Roomer descended. In perfectly-cut tan alpaca suits, horn-rimmed glasses and discreet panamas, they were innocuousness personified. Lord Worth said: 'Mitchell and Roomer. Scientists – geologists and seismologists.' He turned to Mitchell and Roomer and said dully: 'They're holding my daughters captive aboard the *Seawitch*.

'Good God!' Mitchell was properly shocked. 'But surely this is the last place – '

'Of course. The unexpected, keeping the necessary one or two steps ahead of the opposition. What is your purpose in coming here?'

'To find new sources of oil. We have a perfectly equipped laboratory here – '

'Your journey has not been necessary. May we search your bag and that of your friend?'

'Have I any option?'

'No.'

'Go ahead.'

'Aaron '

149

Aaron carried out a quick examination of Mitchell's bag. 'Clothes. Some scientific books and scientific instruments. Is all.'

Dr Greenshaw clambered down the ladder, reached up and relieved the pilot of various bags and boxes. Durand looked at the doctor and said: 'Who the hell is he?'

'Dr Greenshaw,' Lord Worth said. 'A highly respected doctor and surgeon. We did expect a certain amount of violence and bloodshed aboard the *Seawitch*. We came prepared. We do have a dispensary and small sick-bay here.'

'Another wasted trip. We hold all the cards, and violence is the last thing we expect May we examine your equipment, Doctor?'

'If you so wish. As a doctor I deal in life and not in death. I have no concealed lethal weapons. The medical code forbids it.' Greenshaw sighed. 'Please search but do not destroy.'

Durand pulled out his walkie-talkie. 'Send one of Palermo's men across here with an electric truck. There's quite a bit of equipment to pick up.' He replaced his walkie-talkie and looked at Mitchell. 'Your hands are shaking. Why?'

'I'm a man of peace,' Mitchell said. He crossed his hands behind his back to conceal the tremor.

Roomer, the only man to recognize the signals, licked his lips and looked at Mitchell in exaggerated, nervous apprehension. Durand said: 'Another hero. I despise cowards.'

Mitchell brought his hands in front of him. The tremor was still there. Durand stepped forward, his right hand swinging back as if to strike Mitchell open-handed, then let his hand fall in disgust, which was, unwittingly, the wisest thing he had ever done. Durand's mind was brutalized to the extent where it was incapable of picking up any psychic signals: had it been so attuned he could not have failed to hear the black wings of the bird of death flapping above his head.

The only person who derived any satisfaction, carefully concealed, from this vignette, was Larsen. Although he had talked to Mitchell on the telephone he had never met him: but he had heard a great deal about him from Lord Worth, more than enough to make him realize that Mitchell would cheerfully have reduced Durand to mincemeat sooner than back down before him. Mitchell had taken only seconds to establish the role he wished to establish – that of the cowardly nonentity who could be safely and contemptuously ignored. Larsen, who was no mean hand at taking care of people himself, felt strangely comforted.

Lord Worth said: 'May I see my daughters?'

Durand considered, then nodded. 'Search him, Aaron.'

Aaron, carefully avoiding Lord Worth's basilisk glare of icy outrage, duly searched. 'He's clean, Mr Durand.'

'Across there.' Durand pointed through the gathering gloom. 'By the side of the platform.'

Lord Worth walked off without a word. The others made their way towards the accommodation quarters. As Lord Worth approached his daughters Heffer barred his way.

'Where do you think you're going, mister?'

'Lord Worth to you.'

Heffer pulled out his walkie-talkie. 'Mr Durand? There's a guy here – '

Durand's voice crackled over the receiver. 'That's Lord Worth. He has been searched and has my permission to speak to his daughters.'

Lord Worth plucked the walkie-talkie from Heffer. 'And would you please instruct this individual to remain outside listening range?'

'You heard, Heffer ' The walkie-talkie went dead

The reunion between father and daughters was a tear-ful and impassioned one, at least on the daughters' side. Lord Worth was all that a doting parent reunited with his kidnapped children shouid have been, but his effusiveness was kept well under control. Marina was the first to notice this.

'Aren't you *glad* to see us again, Daddy?'

Lord Worth hugged them both and said simply· 'You two are my whole life. If you don't know that by this time, you will never know it.'

'You've never said that before.' Even in the deepening dusk it was possible to see the sheen of tears in Melinda's eyes.

'I did not think it necessary. I thought you always knew. Perhaps I'm a remiss parent, perhaps still too much the reserved Highlander. But all my billions aren't worth a lock of your black hair, Marina, or a lock of your red hair, Melinda.'

'Titian, Daddy, titian. How often must I tell you?' Melinda was openly crying now.

It was Marina, always the more shrewd and perceptive of the two, who put her finger on it. 'You aren't surprised to see us, Daddy, are you? You *knew* we were here '

'Of course I knew '

'How?'

'My agents,' Lord Worth said loftily, 'lie thick upon the ground.'

'And what is going to happen now?'

Lord Worth was frank. 'I'm damned if I know.'

'We saw three other men come off the helicopter Didn't recognize them – getting too dark '

'One was a Dr Greenshaw. Excellent surgeon '

Melinda said: 'What do you want a surgeon for?'

'Don't be silly What does anyone want a surgeon

152

for? You think we're going to hand over the *Seawitch* on a plate?'

'And the other two?'

'You don't know them. You've never heard of them. And if you do meet them you will give no indication that you recognize them or have ever seen them before.'

Marina said: 'Michael and John.'

'Yes. Remember – you've never seen them before.'

'We'll remember,' the girls said almost in chorus. Their faces were transformed. Marina said: 'But they'll be in great danger. Why are they here?'

'Something to do, I understand, with their stated intent of taking you back home.'

'How are they going to do that?'

Again Lord Worth was frank. 'I don't know. If they know, they wouldn't tell me. They've become bossy, very bossy. Watch me like a hawk. Won't even let me near my own blasted phone.' The girls refrained from smiling, principally because Lord Worth didn't seem particularly perturbed. 'Mitchell, especially, seems in a very tetchy mood.' Lord Worth spoke with some relish. 'Near as a whisker killed Durand inside the first minute. Would have, too, if you weren't held hostage. Well, let's go to my suite. I've been to Washington and back. Long, tiring day. I need refreshment.'

Durand went into the radio room, told the regular operator that his services would not be required until further notice and that he was to return to his quarters and remain there. The operator left. Durand, himself an expert radio operator, raised the *Georgia* within a minute and was speaking to Cronkite thirty seconds later.

'Everything under control on the *Seawitch*. We have the two girls here and Lord Worth himself.'

'Excellent.' Cronkite was pleased, and sounded it.

Everything was going his way, but then, he had expected nothing else. 'Lord Worth bring anyone with him?'

'Apart from the pilot, three people. A doctor – surgeon, rather – and he seems genuine enough. Lord Worth appears to have expected some blood to be spilt. I'll check his credentials in Florida in a few minutes. Also, two technicians – seismologists, or something of that kind. Genuine and harmless – even the sight of a slung machine-pistol gives them a severe attack of St Vitus's dance. All are unarmed.'

'So no worries?'

'Yes. Three. Lord Worth has a squad of about twenty men aboard. They have the look of trained killers about them, and I'm pretty certain they're all ex-military personnel. They have to be because of my second worry – Lord Worth has eight dual-purpose anti-aircraft guns bolted on to the platform.'

'The hell he has!'

'I'm afraid so. He also has piles of mines lining the sides of the platform. Now we know who broke into the Mississippi naval armoury last night. And the third problem is that we're far too thin on the ground. There's only myself and four others to watch everybody. Some of us have to sleep sometime. I need reinforcements and I need them quickly.'

'You'll have over twenty arriving at dawn tomorrow morning. The relief rig crew are due in then. A man called Gregson – you'll recognize him by the biggest red beard you ever saw – will be in charge.'

'I can't wait that long. I need reinforcements now. You have your chopper on the *Georgia*.'

'And what do you think I carry aboard the *Georgia*? An army of reinforcements?' Cronkite paused, then went on reluctantly: 'I can spare eight men, no more.'

'They have radar aboard.'

154

'Not unheard of. What does it matter? You're in charge.'

'Yes, Mr Cronkite. But your own golden rule: never take a chance.'

'When you get the word that our helicopter has taken off, neutralize it.'

'Destroy the radar cabin?'

'No. We'll almost certainly want to use it when we've completely taken over. The scanner will be on top of the drilling derrick. Right?'

'Right.'

'It's a simple mechanical job to stop it from turning. All it needs is someone with a spanner and a head for heights. Now tell me exactly where Lord Worth's hard men are quartered. Gregson will require this information.'

Durand told him what he wanted to know and hung up.

The dispensary/sick-bay and the laboratory were next to each other. Mitchell and Roomer were helping Dr Greenshaw to unpack his very considerable amount of medical equipment. They were, understandably, not unguarded, but Aaron and his Schmeisser were on watch on the two outside doors. Aaron could not have been accused of being in a very alert or trigger-ready state of mind. In fact, he regarded his vigil as being close to pointless. He had been present along with Durand when the three men had disembarked from the helicopter, and had formed the same opinion of them as his boss had done.

In the sick-bay Dr Greenshaw up-ended and removed the false bottom of one of his medical supply boxes. With a gingerly and patently nervous apprehension he removed two waistband holsters, two Smith & Wesson .38s, two silencers and two spare magazines. Wordlessly, Mitchell and Roomer buckled on the weaponry. Dr Greenshaw, a

155

man, as they were discovering, of a genuinely devout turn of mind, said: 'I only hope no one discovers you wearing those pistols.'

Roomer said: 'We appreciate your concern, Doctor. But don't worry about us.'

'I wasn't worrying about you.' Dr Greenshaw assumed his most sombre expression. 'A good Christian can also pray for the souls of the ungodly '

A long distance away the meeting of ten were again assembled at Lake Tahoe. At the former meeting the atmosphere had been hopeful, forceful, determined and confident that things would go their way, spuriously motivated by their expressed intent to avert a third world war. On this evening the spirit – if that was the word - of the meeting had changed 180 degrees. They were depressed, vacillating, uncertain and wholly lacking in confidence – especially as their allegedly humanitarian attempts to prevent the outbreak of war looked like having precisely the opposite effect.

Again, as it was his holiday home, Benson was hosting the meeting. But this time Benson was also undoubtedly the man in charge. Opening the discussion, he said: 'We, gentlemen, are in trouble. Not just simple, plain trouble but enormous trouble that could bring us all down. It stems from two facts – we under-estimated Lord Worth's extraordinary power and we over-estimated Cronkite's ability to handle the situation with a suitable degree of discretion and tact. I admit that I was responsible for introducing Cronkite to you, but on the other hand you were unanimous in your belief that Cronkite was the only man to handle the job. And we were not aware that Cronkite's detestation of Lord Worth ran to the extent of a virulent and irresponsible hatred.

'I have friends in the Pentagon, not important ones but

ones that matter. The Pentagon, normally, like any other department of State, leaks secrets as though through a broken sieve. This time I had to pay twenty thousand dollars to a stenographer and the same to a cypher clerk which, for a pair of comparatively lowly-paid government employees, represents a pretty fair return for a few hours' work.

'First, everything is known about our previous meeting here, every word and sentiment that was expressed and the identities of all of us.' Benson paused and looked round the room, partly to allow time for the damning enormity of this information to sink in, partly to make it clear that he expected to be recompensed for his very considerable outlay.

Mr A, one of the vastly powerful Arabian Gulf potentates, said: 'I thought our security here was one hundred per cent. How could anyone have known of our presence?'

'No external agency was involved. I have good friends in California Intelligence. Their interest in us is zero. Nor was the FBI involved. For that to have happened we'd have had to commit some crime and then cross State lines. Neither of those have we done. And before we met last time I had an electronics expert in to check not only this room but the entire house for bugs. There were none.'

Mr A said: 'Perhaps *he* planted a bug?'

'Impossible. Apart from the fact that he's an old friend of immaculate reputation, I was with him all the time, a fact that did not prevent me from calling in a second expert.'

Patinos, the Venezuelan, said: 'We give you full marks for security. That leaves only one possibility. One of us here is a traitor.'

'Yes.'

'Who?'

'I have no idea. We shall probably never know.'

Mr A stroked his beard 'Mr Corral here lives very close to Lord Worth, no?'

Corral said: 'Thank you very much'

Benson said· 'Intelligent men don't make so obvious a link.'

'As you said on our previous meeting, I'm the only person who has no declared interest in being here.' Borosoff seemed quietly relaxed. 'I could be your man.'

'It's a point but one which I don't accept. Whether you are here to stir up trouble for the United States may or may not be the case. Again it comes down to the factor of intelligence.' Benson was being disarmingly frank. 'You could be, and probably are, a Soviet agent. But top agents are never caught in the role of *agent provocateur*. I am not complimenting you on your unquestioned intelligence. I prefer to rely on simple common sense.' Benson, who appeared to have developed a new maturity and authority, looked around the company. 'Every word spoken here will doubtless be relayed to either Lord Worth or the State Department. It no longer matters. We are here to set right whatever wrongs for which we may have been – however unwittingly, I may say – responsible.

'We know that a Russian missile craft and a Russian-built Cuban submarine are closing in on the *Seawitch*. We also know that a Venezuelan destroyer is doing the same. What you don't know is that counter-measures are being taken. My information and the source is impeccable – is that Lord Worth was today closeted with Belton, the Secretary of State, in Washington. My further information is that Belton was only partially convinced of Lord Worth's statement of suspicion. He was, un-fortunately,wholly convinced when the news came through of Cronkite's irresponsible folly in kidnapping Lord Worth's two daughters As a result a United States cruiser and a destroyer, both armed with the most sophisticated weaponry, have moved out into the Gulf of Mexico. An American nuclear submarine is already patrolling those waters. Another American vessel is already shadowing your destroyer, Mr Patinos: your destroyer, with its vastly inferior detecting equipment, is wholly unaware of this. Additionally, at a Louisiana air-base, a squadron of supersonic fighter-bombers is on instant alert.

'The Americans are no longer in any mood to play around. My information is that they are prepared for a showdown and are prepared for the eyeball-to-eyeball confrontation which John Kennedy had with Khrushchev over Cuba. The Russians, clearly, would never risk a local nuclear confrontation where the home territory advantages are so overwhelmingly American. Neither side would dream of mounting a pre-emptive strike over the issue of a few pennies on a barrel of oil. But if the hot line between Washington and Moscow begins to burn, national prestige will make it difficult for either side to back down until they arrive at a face-saving formula which could take quite some time and would, much worse, generate overwhelming world-wide publicity. This would inevitably involve us. So I would advise you, Mr Borosoff and Mr Patinos, to call off your dogs of war before that hot line starts burning. That way, and only by that way, can we survive with our good names left unbesmirched. I blame neither of you gentlemen. You may have given the nod to Cronkite but you did not reckon on the possibility that Cronkite would carry matters to such ridiculous lengths. Please, please believe me that the Americans will not hesitate to blast your ships out of the water.'

Oil ministers do not become oil ministers because they are mentally retarded. Patinos smiled a smile of wry resignation. 'I do not relish the thought of personal ruin.

Nor do I relish the thought of becoming a scapegoat for my government.' He looked across at Borosoff. 'We call off the dogs of war?'

Borosoff nodded. 'Back to their kennels, and no alas. I wish to return to my Russia and this will give me great standing for they will not have to lose face in the world.'

Mr A leaned back in his chair. His relief was manifest. Well, that would seem to cover that.'

'It covers most of it,' Benson said. 'But not all. Another very unpleasant and potentially terrifying crime occurred this afternoon. I heard of it only an hour ago, and it will be the hottest topic in the nation tonight. I only hope to God that, although we were in no way responsible for it, we won't be implicated in it. A place called the "Netley Rowan Armoury" was broken into this afternoon. It's supposed to be just another armoury insofar as the public is concerned and so, mainly, it is. But it's also a TNW armoury. "TNW" means "tactical nuclear weapons". Two of them were stolen in the break-in, and appear to have vanished without trace.'

'God above!' The expression and tone of the man from Honduras accurately reflected the shocked feelings of all around the table 'Cronkite?'

'My life on it. No proof, naturally, but who the hell else?'

Corral said: 'No disrespect to Mr Borosoff here, but couldn't the Russians, say, have been seeking a prototype?'

Benson looked as weary as his voice sounded. 'The Russians already have God knows how many of those things. It's public knowledge that they have thousands of them deployed along the border between the Warsaw Pact countries and Nato, many of them, it is suspected, more sophisticated than ours. The Russians need our TNWs the way they need bows and arrows.' Borosoff, despite the anxiety he shared with the others, permitted himself the ghost of a smile of complacency. 'Cronkite. The man's running wild.'

Mr A said: 'You think he's so totally crazed as to use a nuclear device against the *Seawitch?*'

'I do not profess to understand the workings of an obviously diseased mind,' Benson said. 'He's capable of anything.'

Patinos said: 'What's this weapon like?'

'I don't know. I phoned the Pentagon, a very senior official there, but even although he's an old friend of mine he refused to release highly classified information. All I know is that it can be used as a land-based time-bomb – I suppose that includes the sea as well – or as an aircraft bomb. We can forget the second use. It can only be used in a limited number of supersonic fighter-bombers, which will already, I suppose, be under the heaviest security guard ever, which would strike me as a super-fluous precaution as there is no chance that Cronkite, even with his obviously wide range of contacts, could know anyone who could fly one of those planes.'

'So what happens?'

'I think we'd better consult an astrologer on that one. All I know is that Cronkite has gone stark raving mad.'

Cronkite, aboard the *Georgia*, would have thought the same of them. He had a job to do and he was doing it to the best of his ability. Had he known of the possible withdrawal of the warships that had sailed from Cuba and Venezuela he would not have been overduly concerned. He had had some vague idea that they might have been useful to him in some way, but he had primarily wished to have them as a cover and a smokescreen. Cronkite's vendetta against Lord Worth was a highly personal and extremely vindictive one, and he wanted no one other than himself to administer the *coup de grâce*. Retribution exacted through the medium of other hands would not do at all.

Meantime, he was well content. He was convinced that the *Seawitch* was in his hands. Come the dawn it would be doubly in his hands. He knew of their defences and radar. The *Starlight*, under Easton, was waiting until full darkness before it moved in for the initial attack, and as rain had been falling steadily for some time now and the lowering sky blotted out the quarter-moon, it promised to be as nearly dark as it ever becomes at sea – it never becomes wholly so as it does on land.

A message was brought to him from the radio office Cronkite glanced at it briefly, picked up the phone to the helipad and reached the pilot in his shelter. 'Ready to go, Wilson?'

'Whenever you say, Mr Cronkite.'

'Then now.' Cronkite made a rheostat switch, and a dull glow of light outlined the helipad, little enough to be sure but enough to let Wilson make a clean take-off. The helicopter made a half-circle, switched on its landing lights and made a smooth landing on the calm waters less than a hundred yards from the stationary *Georgia*

Cronkite called the radar room 'You have him on the screen?'

'Yes, sir He's making an instrument approach on our radar '

'Let me know when he's about three miles out.'

Less than a minute later the operator gave him the word. Cronkite turned the rheostat to full, and the helipad became brilliantly illuminated

A minute later a helicopter, landing lights on, appeared from the north through the driving rain. Just over another minute later it touched down as delicately as a moth, an understandable precaution by the pilot in view of the cargo he was carrying. The fuelling hoses were connected immediately. The door opened and three men descended – the alleged Colonel Farquharson, Lieutenant-Colonel Dewings and Major Breckley who had been responsible for the Netley Rowan Armoury break-in. They helped unload two large, double-handed and obviously very heavy suitcases. Cronkite, with suitable admonitions as to delicacy in handling, showed crew members where to stow the cases in shelter.

Within ten minutes the helicopter was on its way back to the mainland. Five minutes after that the *Georgia*'s own helicopter had returned and all the helipad lights were switched off

chapter

8

It was due only to the most cruel ill-luck and the extremely jittery state of Durand's nerves that John Roomer and Melinda Worth found themselves the first patients in Dr Greenshaw's sick-bay.

Durand was in a highly apprehensive state of mind, a mood that transferred itself all too easily to his four subordinates. Although he held control of the *Seawitch* he was acutely aware that his hold was a tenuous one: he had not bargained on finding Palermo and his cut-throats on board, and even though he held the master keys to both the Occidental and Oriental quarters in his pocket – the drilling crew was in the former quarters, Palermo and his men in the latter – he was well aware that there were far too many windows in both quarters and he didn't have the men to cover every possible exit. He had broadcast a message over the external loud-hailer that anyone found on the platform would be shot on sight, and had two men on constant patrol round the Oriental quarters - he had no fear of the unarmed drilling rig crew – and another two constantly patrolling the platform. He had no fear of Lord Worth, his seismologists and the girls – as sources of danger he held them in contempt. Besides, they were unarmed Even so, the two men patrolling the platform had been instructed to do so in such a fashion as to make sure that at least one had an eye on the doors to the suite of Lord Worth, the laboratory

and the sick-bay, all three of which had inter communi
cating doors

Tragically, no one inside those three places had heard
the warning broadcast – and this, ironically, because
Lord Worth was not above indulging in what he regarded
as the bare minimum of basic creature comforts. Oil rigs
can be uncommonly noisy places and those quarters he
had heavily insulated.

Mitchell had been in his tiny cubicle off the laboratory
at the time, reading the plan of the lay-out of the *Seawitch*
over and over again until he was certain that he could
have found his way around the *Seawitch* blindfold. This
had taken him about twenty minutes. It was in the fifth
minute of his studying that the shots had been fired but
again, because of the soundproofing, the firing had not
reached him. He had just put the plans away in a drawer
when his door opened and Marina entered. She was
white-faced and shaking and her face was streaked with
tears. As soon as she reached him he put his arms round
her and she grabbed him as if he were the last straw in the
middle of the Pacific.

'Why weren't you there?' she sobbed. 'Why weren't you
there? You could have stopped them. You could have
saved them!'

Mitchell took no time out to dwell upon the injustices
of life. He said gently: 'Stopped what? Saved whom?'

'Melinda and John. They've been terribly hurt.'

'How?'

'Shot.'

'Shot? I heard nothing.'

'Of course you heard nothing. This area is all soundproofed That's why Melinda and John didn't hear the
broadcast warning.'

'Broadcast warning? Tell it to me slowly.'

So she told him as slowly and coherently as she could.

There had been such a warning but it had gone unheard in Lord Worth's suite. The rain had stopped, at least temporarily, and when Mitchell had retired to study the plans Melinda and Roomer had elected to go for a stroll. They had been wandering around the foot of the drilling rig, where most of the lights had been turned off since Durand had ordered the abandonment of drilling, and it was there that they had been gunned down without warning.

' "Terribly hurt", you said. How badly hurt?'

'I'm not sure. Dr Greenshaw is operating in the sick-bay. I'm not a coward, you know that, but there was so much blood that I didn't want to look.'

Arrived in the sick-bay, Mitchell could hardly blame her. Melinda and Roomer lay in adjacent cots and both were saturated with blood. Melinda already had her left shoulder heavily bandaged. Roomer had bandages swathed round his neck and Dr Greenshaw was working on his chest.

Lord Worth, his face a mask of bitter fury, was sitting in a chair. Durand, his face a mask of nothingness, was standing by the doorway. Mitchell looked speculatively at both, then spoke to Dr Greenshaw. 'What have you been able to determine so far, Doctor?'

'Would you listen to him?' Roomer's voice was a hoarse whisper and his face creased with near-agony. 'Never think of asking us how *we* feel.'

'In a moment. Well, Doctor?'

'Lady Melinda's left shoulder-blade is in a pretty bad way. I've extracted the bullet, but she needs immediate surgery. I'm a surgeon, but I'm not an orthopaedic surgeon, and that's what she must have. Roomer hasn't been quite so lucky. He got hit twice. The one through the neck missed his carotid artery by a whisker, but the bullet passed straight through and there's no worry there. The chest wound is serious. Not fatal but very serious. The bullet struck the left lung, no doubt about that, but the internal bleeding isn't that much, so I think it's a nick, no more. The trouble is, I think the bullet is lodged against the spine '

'He can wiggle his toes?'

Roomer moaned. 'My God, what sympathy

'He can But the bullet should be removed as soon as possible I could do it but I have no X-ray equipment here I'll give them both blood transfusions in a moment.'

'Shouldn't they be flown to hospital as soon as possible?'

'Of course '

Mitchell looked at Durand. 'Well?'

'No.'

'But it wasn't their fault. They didn't hear the warning.'

'Their bad luck. There's no way I'll fly them ashore Think I want a battalion of US Marines out here in a few hours?'

'If they die it'll be your fault.'

'Everybody's got to die sometime.' Durand left, slamming the door behind him.

'Dear, dear.' Roomer tried to shake his head then winced at the pain in his neck. 'He shouldn't have said that '

Mitchell turned to Lord Worth. 'You can be of great help, sir. Your suite is in direct contact with the radio room, of course. Can you actually hear what is being said in the radio room?'

'No bother. Two switches and I can hear both sides of any conversation, either on the telephone, earphones or wall-receivers.'

'Please go and do so and don't stop listening for a second.' He looked at the two patients on the cots. 'We'll have them airborne for hospital within the half-hour '

'How can that be possible?'

'I don't know.' Mitchell sounded vague. 'I dare say we'll think of something.'

Lord Worth left. Mitchell pulled out a slender pencil flashlight and started to flick it on and off in apparent aimlessness. His complexion had gone pale and the hands that held the pencil light trembled slightly. Marina looked at him first uncomprehendingly, then in dismay, finally in something approaching contempt. Incredulously, she said: 'You're frightened.'

'Your gun?' Mitchell said to Roomer.

'When they went off for help I managed to drag myself a bit nearer the edge. I unclipped the belt and threw the lot over the side.'

'Good lad. So we're still in the clear.' He seemed to become aware of the tremor in his hands, put away his flashlight and thrust his hands into his pockets. He said to Melinda: 'Who shot you?'

'A pair of very unpleasant characters called Kowenski and Rindler. We've had trouble with them before.'

'Kowenski and Rindler,' Mitchell repeated. He left the sick-bay.

Marina said, half in sadness, half in bitterness: 'My idol with the feet of clay.'

Roomer said huskily: 'Put out the light and then put out the light.'

'What did you say?'

'I didn't say it. Chap called Othello. That's the trouble with you millionaire's daughters. Illiterate. First Mitchell puts out the lights. He's got cat's eyes. He can see in almost total darkness where an ordinary man is blind. Did you know that?'

'No.'

'Puts him at a tremendous advantage. And then he

168

extinguishes another kind of light.'

'I know what you mean and I don't believe you. I saw him shaking.'

'You poor, silly, stupid, foolish ninny. You don't deserve him.'

She stared at him in disbelief. 'What did you say?'

'You heard me.' Roomer sounded tired and the doctor was looking at him in disapproval. He went on in a sombre voice: 'Kowenski and Rindler are dead men. They have minutes to live. He loves your sister almost as much as he does you, and I've been his closest friend and partner since we were kids. Mitchell looks after his own.' He smiled faintly. 'I'm afraid he takes care of things in a rather final way.'

'But he was shaking – only cowards shake.' Her voice was now lacking in conviction.

'He's afraid of nothing that lives. As for the shaking – he's a throw-back to the old Scandinavian berserker. He's just trying to contain his fury. He usually smiles. As for being a coward, quite a number of people have thought that of him – probably their last thought on earth.' He smiled. 'You're shaking now.'

She said nothing.

Roomer said: 'There's a cupboard in the vestibule Bring what you find there.'

She looked at him uncertainly, left, and returned in a few minutes carrying a pair of shoes. She held them at arm's length and from the look of horror on her face might have been holding a cobra.

Roomer said: 'Mitchell's?'

'Yes.'

'Better return them. He'll be requiring them quite soon.'

When she came back Melinda said: 'Do you really think you could marry a man who kills people?'

Marina shivered and said nothing. Roomer said

sardonically: 'Better than marrying a coward, I should think.'

In the generator room Mitchell found what he wanted right away – a breaker marked 'Deck Lights'. He pulled down the lever and stepped out on to the now darkened platform. He waited a half-minute until his eyes adjusted themselves to the darkness, then moved in the direction of the derrick crane where he could hear two men cursing in far from muted voices. He approached on soundless stockinged feet until he was less than two yards away. Still soundlessly, he laid his pencil flash on top of the barrel of the Smith & Wesson and slid forward the flash switch.

The two men swung round in remarkably swift unison, hands reaching for their guns.

Mitchell said: 'You know what this is, don't you?'

They knew. The deep-bluish sheen of a silenced .38 is not readily mistakable for a pop-gun. Their hands stopped reaching for their guns. It was, to say the least, rather unnerving to see an illuminated silenced gun and nothing but blackness beyond it.

'Clasp your hands behind your necks, turn round and start walking.'

They walked until they could walk no more for the good reason that they had reached the end of the platform Beyond that lay nothing but the 200-foot drop to the Gulf of Mexico.

Mitchell said: 'Keep your hands even more tightly clasped and turn round.'

They did so. 'You are Kowenski and Rindler?'

There was no reply.

'You are the two who gunned down Lady Melinda and Mr Roomer?'

Again there was no reply. Vocal chords can become paralysed when the mind is possessed of the irrevocable

170

certainty that one is but one step, one second removed from eternity. Mitchell squeezed the trigger twice and was walking away before the dead men had hit the waters of the Gulf. He had taken only four steps when a flash-light struck him in the face.

'Well, well, if it isn't clever-clever Mitchell, the scaredy scientist.' Mitchell couldn't see the man – and undoubtedly the gun behind the flash – but he had no difficulty in recognizing the voice of Heffer, the one with the sharp nose and rodent-like teeth. '*And* carrying a silenced gun. Whatever have we been up to, Mr Mitchell?'

Heffer had made the classic blunder of all incompetent would-be assassins. He should have shot Mitchell on sight and then asked the questions. Mitchell flicked on his pencil torch and spun it upwards, where it spun around like a demented firefly. Heffer would have been less than human not to have had the automatic and instinctive reaction of glancing upwards while either his conscious or subconscious mind speculated as to what the hell Mitchell was up to: whichever it was, the speculation was of very brief duration indeed, because Heffer was dead before the flash fell back on to the platform.

Mitchell picked up the flash, still surprisingly working, dragged Heffer by the heels to join his friends at the bottom of the Gulf, returned to the sick-bay vestibule, donned his shoes and entered the sick-bay itself. Dr Greenshaw had both his patients on blood transfusion.

Roomer looked at his watch. 'Six minutes. What took you so long?'

A plainly unnerved Marina looked at Roomer, half in disbelief, half in stupefaction.

'Well, I'm sorry.' Mitchell actually managed to sound apologetic 'I had the misfortune to run into Heffer on the way back.'

'You mean he had the misfortune to run into you And

where are our friends?"

'I'm not rightly sure.'

'I understand.' Roomer sounded sympathetic. 'It's difficult to estimate the depth of the water hereabouts.'

'I could find out. It hardly seems to matter. Dr Greenshaw, you have stretchers? Complete with straps and so forth?' Greenshaw nodded. 'Please prepare them. Let them stay where they are meantime. Blood transfusions can be carried on in flight?'

'That's no problem. I assume you want me to accompany them?'

'If you would be so kind. I know it's asking an awful lot but, after you've handed them over to the competent medical authorities, I'd like you to return.'

'It will be a pleasure. I am now in my seventieth year and thought there was nothing fresh left in life for me to experience. I was wrong.'

Marina stared at them in disbelief. All three men seemed calm and relaxed. Melinda appeared to have dropped off into a coma but she was merely, in fact, under heavy sedation. Marina said with conviction: 'You're all mad.'

Mitchell said: 'That's what the inmate of a lunatic asylum says of the outside world, and he may well be right. However, that's hardly the point at issue. You, Marina, will be accompanying the others on the trip back to Florida. There you will be perfectly safe – your father will ensure that the most massive security guard ever mounted will be there. No president in history will ever have been so well protected.'

'How splendid. I love being made a fuss of, being the centre of attraction. However, master-mind, there's just one small flaw in your reasoning. I'm not going. I'm staying with my father'

'That's exactly the point I'm going to discuss with him now.'

'You mean you're going out to kill someone else?'

Mitchell held out his hands, fingers splayed. They could have been carved from marble.

'Later,' Roomer said. 'He appears to have some other things on his mind at the moment.'

Mitchell left. Marina turned furiously on Roomer 'You're just as bad as he is.'

'I'm a sick man. You mustn't upset me.'

'You and his berserker moods. He's just a killer.'

Roomer's face went very still. 'I don't look forward to the prospect of having a mentally retarded person as a sister-in-law.'

She was shocked and the shock showed. Her voice was a whisper. 'I don't really know you, do I?'

'No. We're the men who walk down the dark side of the streets. Somebody has to look after the people on the dark side. We do it. Do you know how much your father offered us to take you home?' Roomer smiled. 'I'm afraid I'm not much good in that department at the moment, but Mike will take care of it.'

'How much did he offer you?'

'Whatever we wanted in the world. A million dollars to take you home? A hundred million if we'd asked for it? Sure.'

'How much did you ask for?' Her face wasn't registering much in the way of expression.

Roomer sighed, which, in the low physical state he felt, wasn't too difficult. 'Poor Mike. To think that he regards you as the pot of gold at the foot of the rainbow. Maybe he'd better get off that rainbow – insubstantial things at the best of times. Poor me, too. I'm going to have to live with you too, even at second hand. Let's be corny. Your father loves you. We love you To pile cliché upon cliché, ᵗhere are some things that can't be bought. Pearls bevond price. Don't make yourself an artificial pearl, Marina. And don't ever again insult us in that fashion. But we have to live on something, so we'll send him a bill.'

'For what?'

'Ammunition expended.'

She crossed to his cot-side, knelt and kissed him. Roomer seemed too weak to resist. Dr Greenshaw was severe. 'Lady Marina, he's not only having a blood transfusion, there's also the factor of blood pressure.'

Roomer said: 'My blood pressure is registering no complaints.'

She kissed him again. 'Is that apology enough?' Roomer smiled and said nothing. ' "Berserker", you said Can anyone stop him when he's like that? Can I ?'

'No. Some day, yes.'

'The one person is you Yes?'

'Yes.'

'You didn't.'

'No.'

'Why?'

'They carried guns.'

'You carry guns.'

'Yes. But we're not evil people who carry guns to do evil things.'

'That's all?'

'No.' He looked across at Melinda. 'You see?'

'Please.'

'If Kowenski and Rindler hadn't been such damned lousy shots, she'd be dead.'

'So you let Michael loose?'

'Yes.'

'You're going to marry her?'

'Yes.'

'Have you asked her?'

'No '

You don't have to Sisters talk.'

'Mike?'

'I don't know, John. I'm a running coward, running scared.'

'Well?'

'He kills.'

'I've killed.'

'He'll kill again?'

'I don't know.'

'John.'

He reached out, took a lock of her gleaming black hair, picked out a single thread. 'That.'

'You mean?'

'Yes.'

'I have to see.' She kicked off her high-heeled shoes.

'So much to learn. Sit.'

She sat on his bed. Dr Greenshaw rolled his eyes heavenwards. She was wearing navy-blue jeans and a white blouse. Roomer reached up and undid the top button of her blouse. She looked at him and said nothing. Roomer said: 'You do the rest. Navy or black jumper.'

She was back in thirty seconds, wearing a navy polo. She looked enquiringly at Roomer, who nodded. She left the sick-bay.

In Lord Worth's living-room he and Mitchell were seated in adjacent armchairs. The wall-speakers were on. When Marina came in Mitchell waved her to urgent silence.

Over the speakers Durand's unmistakable voice sounded testy. 'All I know is that the deck lights went out some minutes ago and came back on a minute ago.' Marina glanced at Mitchell, who nodded. 'But you've all the light you need to land.'

'Have you neutralized the radar scanner yet?'

Marina had never heard the voice before, but the tightening of Lord Worth's lip showed that Cronkite's voice was no stranger to him.

'It hardly seems necessary now.'

'It was your idea. Do it. We'll leave in ten minutes, then there'll be about fifteen minutes' flying time.'

' "*We'll* leave"? That mean you're coming too?'

'No. I've more important things to do.' There was a click: Cronkite had ceased to transmit.

Lord Worth said uneasily: 'I wonder what that devious devil means by that?'

'We'll just have to find out the hard way.' Mitchell looked at Marina. 'Where are your shoes?'

She smiled sweetly. 'I'm a quick study. Shoes make too much noise out on the platform.

'You're not going out on any platform.'

'I am. There are gaps in my education I want to see how killers operate.'

Mitchell said in irritation: 'I'm not going to kill anyone Go get your bag packed. You'll be leaving soon.'

'I'm not leaving.'

'Why?'

'Because I want to stay with Daddy – and with you. Don't you think that natural?'

'You're leaving if I have to tie you up.'

'You can't tie my tongue up. Wouldn't the law just love to know where the guns stolen from the Mississippi armoury are?'

Lord Worth looked slightly stunned. 'You'd do that to me? Your own father?'

'You'd tie me up and force me aboard that helicopter – Your own daughter?'

'Talk about logic.' Mitchell shook his head. 'With respects to Lord Worth, he appears to have fathered a nutcase. If you think – '

176

The wall-speakers crackled again It was Cronkite's voice 'Well, don't just hang around. Stop that radar'

'How?' It was Aaron and he sounded aggrieved. 'Do you expect me to climb that damned drilling rig –

'Don't be stupid. Go to the radar room. There's a red lever switch just above the console. Pull it down.'

'That I can do.' Aaron sounded relieved. They heard the sound of a door closing. Mitchell kicked off his shoes, turned off the lights in the living-room and eased the door open a crack. Aaron, his back already to them, was heading for the radar room. He reached it, opened the door and passed inside. Mitchell moved after him, pulling out his silenced gun and held it in his left hand. A soft voice behind him said: 'I thought you were right-handed?'

Mitchell didn't even bother to curse He said in a resigned whisper: 'I am.'

Aaron was just pulling the red lever when Mitchell made his soundless entrance He said· 'Don't turn round'

Aaron didn't turn round

'Clasp your hands behind your neck. then turn and come here.'

Aaron turned. 'Mitchell!'

'Please don't try anything clever. I've already had to kill three of your friends tonight. A fourth isn't going to give me a sleepless night. Stop right there and turn again.'

Aaron did as he was told. Mitchell withdrew his right hand from his coat pocket. The braided leather strap attached to his wrist by a thong was no more than five inches long, but when it struck Aaron with considerable force and accuracy above and behind the right ear it was apparent that five inches was quite long enough Mitchell caught him as he fell and eased him to the deck

'Did you have to do that? – ' Marina choked and stopped speaking as Mitchell's hand clamped itself none too gently over her mouth. She flinched as he shook the strap before her eyes.

'Keep your voice down.' The whisper was intentionally savage. He knelt over Aaron, removed and pocketed his gun.

'Did you have to do that?' she said in a low voice. 'You could have tied him up and gagged him.'

'When I require advice from ignorant amateurs I'll turn to you immediately. I haven't time for *fol-de-rols*. He'll just have a half-hour's peaceful rest, and then all he'll need is an aspirin.'

'And now?'

'Durand.'

'Why?'

'Ninny.'

'I'm getting tired of people calling me "ninny". John just called me that. He also said I was mentally retarded and an artificial pearl.'

'No shrewder judge of character than our John,' Mitchell said approvingly. 'If Aaron doesn't return Durand will come looking for him. Then he'll get on the radio-phone and stop the helicopter flight.'

'Well, that's what you want, isn't it?'

'No.'

He switched off the light and walked away, Marina following. Mitchell stopped outside the entrance to Lord Worth's sitting-room

'Get inside. You're both an irritation and a liability. I can't function properly with you around. Heroines I can do without '

'I promise you I won't say a word. I promise – '

He caught her by the arm and thrust her forcibly inside. Lord Worth looked up in mild surprise. Mitchell said: 'I will hold you personally responsible, Lord Worth, if you allow this pesky daughter of yours outside that door again

More, I'm dimming the deck lights. Any unauthorized person seen moving around the platform will be shot on sight. That is my promise, and you'd better believe it. This is no place for children who want to play games.' The door closed behind him

'Well!' Marina sat down and gripped her hands together. 'What kind of husband do you think *he* would make?'

'A perfectly splendid one, I should imagine. Look, my dear, one of Mitchell's outstanding assets is a hair-trigger reaction. You blunt it. And you know damn well how he feels about you – your presence just constitutes an additional worry at a time when he can least afford either. A wife doesn't accompany her husband down a coal mine or on a wartime bombing mission. And Mitchell is much more of a loner than such people are.'

She attempted something between a glower and a scowl, but her beautiful face really wasn't made for it so she settled for a rueful smile, rose and replenished his glass of malt whisky.

Mitchell removed the gun and two large keys from the pockets of an unconscious Durand, made his way to the main entrance to the Oriental quarters, opened the door and switched on the corridor lights.

'Commander Larsen,' he called out. 'Palermo.'

Doors opened and the two men were with him in a few seconds. Larsen said: 'Mitchell! What the hell are you doing here?'

'Just a harmless seismologist taking his constitutional.'

'But didn't you hear the broadcast warning – anyone seen on the platform to be shot on sight?'

'That's past. One piece of bad news, two of good. Bad first. Roomer and Miss Melinda didn't hear the warning those quarters are sound-insulated. So they took a walk.

Both were hurt quite badly. Melinda has a shattered left shoulder, Roomer was shot through the neck and chest. The doctor thinks the bullet is lodged against his spine. We must get them to hospital and quick. Who's Lord Worth's personal pilot?'

'Chambers,' Larsen said.

'Get one of your men to have him refuel his machine. The good news: Durand is in the radio room, his number two, fellow called Aaron, is in the radar room. Both are unconscious.' He looked at Palermo. 'When they come to – it'll be some time yet – could you have them looked after with loving care and attention?'

'Our pleasure.'

Larsen said: 'Durand had three other men.'

'They're dead.'

'You?'

'Yes.'

'We didn't hear any shooting.'

Mitchell gave them a brief sight of his silenced .38. Larsen looked thoughtful. 'Lord Worth talked quite a bit about you. I used to think he was exaggerating.'

'The other bit of good news. Cronkite is sending some reinforcements by helicopter – not many, I believe, eight or nine – and they should be taking off about now. A fifteen minutes' flight, I gather, so I reckon that Cronkite's boat is just somewhere below the horizon, below our radar sweep.'

Palermo brightened 'We blast this chopper out of the sky?'

'My original thought, I must admit. But let's try to play it clever and lull him into some sort of sense of false security. I suggest we let them land, then take them. We'll have their leader report to Cronkite that all is well.'

What if he refuses? Or tries to shout a warning?'

We'll write out his script. If he deviates one word I'll

shoot him. Silencer. Cronkite will hear nothing.'

'He could hear the man scream.'

'When a .38 enters the base of your skull and travels upwards at forty-five degrees you don't tend to scream much.'

'You mean you'd kill him?' While not exactly incredulous, Larsen was obviously taken aback.

'Yes. Then we'd line up number two. We shouldn't have too much trouble with him.'

Larsen said with some feeling: 'When Lord Worth talked of you he didn't tell me the half of it.'

'Another thing. I want that helicopter. We'll fake up a tale that the engine failed above the helipad, crash-landed and will take some hours to repair. Always useful to have another helicopter around but, more importantly, I want to deprive Cronkite of the use of his. He looked at Palermo. 'I take it that the reception committee can be safely left in your hands.'

'You sure can. Any suggestions?'

'Well, I'm a bit diffident about lecturing an expert like yourself.'

'You know me?'

'I used to be a cop. The rig is loaded with portable search-lights. They'll head for the administration buildings. I'd keep in hiding, switch off the deck lights and turn on the search-lights when they are, say, thirty yards away. They'll be blind and won't be able to see you.'

'You can't cater for nutcases.'

'I'll bet *you* can.' Mitchell smiled briefly at him, cop to crook. He said to Larsen 'I have a feeling that Lord Worth would like to confer with his rig boss.'

'Yes.' They walked away as Palermo was already giving rapid instructions to his men. 'Lord Worth know what you're up to?'

'I haven't had time Anyway, I wouldn't tell Lord

181

Worth how to make a billion out of oil.'

'A point.' They stopped briefly by the radio room Larsen gazed at the crumpled form of Durand, half in appreciation, half in regret. 'What a beautiful sight. Wish it had been me, though.'

'I'll bet Durand – when he awakes · doesn't. Plastic surgeons come high.'

They made their next brief stop at the sick-bay. He looked at a still comatose Melinda and a wide-awake Roomer, and his massive fists clenched. Roomer smiled. 'I know. But you're too late. How deep's the water here?'

'Nine hundred feet.'

'Then you'd require a diving-bell to get your hands round the throats of those responsible. And how are things with you, Commander Larsen? You can see how things are with us.'

'I've been resting. Mitchell here has been rather more active. Apart from the three men at the bottom of the Gulf, he's also deprived me of the pleasure of beating the living daylights out of Durand. Aaron isn't feeling too well either.'

Roomer said apologetically: 'He doesn't go in much for diplomacy. So the *Seawitch* is in our hands?'

'For the moment.'

'For the moment?'

'Do you see a man like Cronkite giving up? So he's lost five men and is probably about to lose another eight or nine. What's that for a man with ten million to play about with? And don't forget his vicious personal vendetta with Lord Worth. If achieving his intent involves the crippling or even the destruction of the *Seawitch*, including all aboard it – well, Cronkite isn't going to be conscience-ridden for all his days – or even for a minute if it comes to that.' He turned to Dr Greenshaw. 'I think it's time you got busy with the stretchers. Could you

spare four of your drilling crew, Commander, to help
have them transferred to the stretchers and then carried
across to the helicopter? I'm afraid, John, that you're
going to have some very unpleasant company on the trip.
Durand and Aaron. Trussed like chickens, of course.'

'Well, thank you very much.'

'I can   occasionally – be as leery as you. I wouldn't
put it past Cronkite to gain access to the *Seawitch*. How
he would do it I haven't the faintest idea, but with a
devious mind a highly-motivated man can accomplish
almost anything he wants. Should he succeed I don't want
Durand and Aaron pointing accusing fingers at me. I
should like to remain an inconspicuous and harmless
seismologist.'

Larsen gave a few orders on the phone, then he and
Mitchell went through to Lord Worth's room. Lord Worth
was on the phone, listening and scowling. Marina looked
at Mitchell with an expression as forbidding as her father's.

'I suppose you've been littering the platform with a
few more dead men?'

'You do me a grave injustice. There's no one left to
kill.' She gave what might have been a tiny shudder and
looked away.

Larsen said: 'The ship is in our hands, Lady Marina.
We're expecting a little more trouble in about ten
minutes, but we can take care of that.'

Lord Worth replaced his receiver. 'What's that?'

'Cronkite is sending some reinforcements by helicopter.
Not many – eight or nine. They'll have no chance. He's
under the impression that Durand is still in charge here.'

'I take it he's not.'

'He's unconscious and very securely bound. So is
Aaron.'

A yearning look came over Lord Worth's face. 'Is
Cronkite coming with them?'

'No.'

'How very unfortunate. And I've just had some more bad news. The *Torbello* has broken down.'

'Sabotage?'

'No. The main fuel supply line to its engine has fractured. Just a temporary stop, though it may take some hours to repair. But there is no cause for worry and half-hourly reports on the state of repairs should be forthcoming.'

Another disturbing point had arisen. No major marine insurance companies or Lloyd's of London had ever heard of the existence of the *Questar*. Even more disturbing, however, was that the Marine Gulf Corporation had reported the disappearance of its seismological survey vessel from Freeport. It was called the *Hammond*.

The US navy had two points of cold comfort to offer. What the United States did with its obsolete submarines was to scrap them or sell them to foreign governments: none had ever fallen into the hands of commercial companies or private individuals. Nor were there any Cousteau-type submersibles along the Gulf Coast.

The telephone call-up bell jangled. Lord Worth switched on the wall-receivers. The radio officer was succinct.

'Helicopter, flying low, due north-west, five miles out.'

'Well, now,' Larsen said, 'this should provide a diversion. Coming, Mitchell?'

'In a moment. I have a little note to write. Remember?'

'The note, of course.' Larsen left. Mitchell penned a brief note in neat printed script that left no room for misinterpretation, folded it in his pocket and went to the door. Lord Worth said: 'Mind if I come along?'

'Well, there'll be no danger, but I think you'd be better occupied in listening for messages from radar, radio, sonar and those monitoring the sensory devices attached to the massive anchoring cables.'

184

'Agreed. And I'll call up the Secretary to see what luck he's had in hauling those damned warships off my back.'

Marina said sweetly: 'If there's no danger I'm coming with you.'

'No.'

'You have a very limited vocabulary, Mr Mitchell.'

'Instead of trying to be a heroine you might try the Florence Nightingale bit – there are two very sick people through there who require their hands held.'

'You're too bossy by half, Michael.'

'In today's idiom, a male chauvinist pig.'

Could you imagine me marrying a person like you?'

'Your imagination is your business. Besides, I've never asked you to.' He left.

'Well!' She looked suspiciously at her father, but Lord Worth had his risibility under complete control. He picked up a phone and asked for the Christmas tree to be opened and the exploratory drilling restarted.

The helicopter was making its landing approach as Mitchell joined Larsen and Palermo and his men in the deep shadows of the accommodation area. The platform lights had been dimmed but the helipad was brightly illuminated. Palermo had six portable search-lights in position. He nodded to Mitchell, then made his un-hurried way to the helipad. He was carrying an envelope in his hand.

The helicopter touched down, the door opened and men with a discouraging assortment of automatic weapons started to disembark. Palermo said: 'I'm Marino. Who's in charge here?'

'Me. Mortensen.' He was a bulky young man in battle fatigues, and looked more like a bright young lieutenant than the thug he undoubtedly was. 'I thought Durand was in charge here?'

'He is. At the moment he's having a brief and painful conversation with Lord Worth. He's waiting for you in Lord Worth's quarters.'

'Why are the deck lights so dim?'

'Voltage drop. Being fixed. The helipads have their own generators.' He pointed. 'Over there.'

Mortensen nodded and led his eight men away. Palermo said: 'Join you in a minute. I have a private message for the pilot from Cronkite.'

Palermo climbed up into the helicopter He greeted the pilot and said: 'I have a message here for you from Cronkite.'

The pilot registered a degree of surprise. 'I was under orders to fly straight back.'

'Won't be long. It appears that Cronkite is anxious to see Lord Worth and his daughters.'

The pilot grinned and took the envelope from Palermo. He opened it, examined both sides of a blank sheet of paper and said: 'What gives?'

'This.' Palermo showed him a gun about the size of a small cannon. 'I can't stand dead heroes.'

The platform lights went out and six search-lights came on. Larsen's stentorian voice carried clearly. 'Throw down your guns. You have no chance.'

One of Mortensen's men suicidally thought different. He flung himself to the platform deck, loosed off a burst of sub-machine-gun fire and successfully killed one of the search-lights. If he felt any sense of gratification it must have been the shortest on record, for he was dead while the shattered glass was still tinkling down on the platform. The other eight men threw down their guns.

Palermo sighed. He said to the pilot: 'See? Dead heroes are no good to anyone. Come along.'

Eight of the nine men, together with the pilot, were shepherded into a windowless store-room and locked inside.

186

The ninth, Mortensen, was taken to the radio room where he was shortly joined by Mitchell. For the occasion Mitchell had changed into a boiler-suit and makeshift hood, which not only effectively masked his face but also muffled his voice. He had no wish to be identified.

He produced the paper on which he had made notes, screwed the muzzle of his .38 into the base of Mortensen's neck, told him to contact Cronkite and read out the message and that the slightest deviation from the script would mean a shattered brain. Mortensen was no fool and in his peculiar line of trade he had looked into the face of death more than once. He made the contact, said all was well, that he and Durand were in complete control of the *Seawitch* but that it might be several hours before the helicopter could return as last-minute engine-failure had damaged the under-carriage. Cronkite seemed reasonably satisfied and hung up.

When Larsen and Mitchell returned to Lord Worth's cabin Lord Worth seemed in a more cheerful frame of mind. The Pentagon had reported that the two naval vessels from Cuba and the one from Venezuela were stopped in the water and appeared to be awaiting instructions. The *Torbello* was on its way again and was expected to arrive in Galveston in ninety minutes. Lord Worth might have felt less satisfied if he'd known that the *Torbello*, shaking in every rivet, seam and plate, was several hundred miles from Galveston, travelling south-west in calm seas. Mulhooney was in no mood to hang around.

Marina said accusingly: 'I heard shots being fired out there '

'Just warning shots in the air,' Mitchell said. 'Frightens the hell out of people '

'You made them all prisoner.

187

Lord Worth said irritably: 'Don't talk nonsense. Now do be quiet. The Commander and I have important matters to discuss.'

'We'll leave,' Mitchell said. He looked at Marina. 'Come and let's see the patients off'

They followed the two stretchers out to the helicopter. They were accompanied by Durand and Aaron – both with their hands lashed behind their backs and on a nine-inch hobble – Dr Greenshaw and one of Palermo's men, a menacing individual with a sawn-off shot-gun who was to ride guard on the captives until they reached the mainland

Mitchell said to Marina: 'Last chance.'

'No '

'We're going to make a great couple,' Mitchell said gloomily 'Monosyllabic is what I mean.'

They said their goodbyes, watched the helicopter lift off and made their way back to Lord Worth's quarters Both he and Larsen were on separate lines, and from the expressions on their faces it was clear that they were less happy with life than they might have been. Both men were trying, with zero effect, to obtain some additional tankerage. There were, in fact, some half-dozen idle tankers on the south and east coast in the 50,000 dw range, but all belonged to the major oil companies who would have gone to the stake sooner than charter any of their vessels to the Worth Hudson Oil Company. The nearest tankers of the required tonnage were either in Britain, Norway or the Mediterranean, and to have brought them across would have involved an intolerable loss of time, not to say money, which last matter lay very close to Lord Worth's heart. He and Larsen had even considered bringing one of their super-tankers into service, but had decided against it. Because of the tankers' huge carrying capacity, the loss in revenue would have been unbearably high. And what had happened to the *Crusader* might even happen to a super-tanker True, they were insured at Lloyd's, but that august firm's marine accident investigators were notoriously, if justifiably, cagey, prudent and thoroughly cautious men, and although they invariably settled any genuine claim they tended to deliberate at length before making any final decision.

Another call came through from the *Torbello*. On course, its estimated time of arrival in Galveston was one hour. Lord Worth said gloomily that they had at least two tankers in operation: they would just have to step up their already crowded schedules.

One half-hour later another message came through from the tanker. One half-hour to Galveston. Lord Worth might have felt less assured had he known that now that dark had fallen the *Starlight*, leaving the *Georgia* where it was, had already moved away in the direction of the *Seawitch*, its engines running on its electrical batteries. Its chances of sonar detection by the *Seawitch* were regarded as extremely small. It carried with it highly skilled divers and an unpleasant assortment of mines, limpet mines and amatol beehives, all of which could be controlled by long-distance radio.

Yet another half-hour passed before the welcome news came through that the tanker *Torbello* was safely berthed in Galveston. Lord Worth said to Larsen that he intended to make an immediate voice-link call to the port authorities in Galveston to ensure the fastest turn-round ever, money no object.

He got his voice-link in just one minute – the Lord Worths of this world are never kept waiting. When he made his customary peremptory demands the harbour-master expressed a considerable degree of surprise.

'I really can't imagine what you are talking about, sir.'

'God damn it, I always know what I'm talking about.'

'Not in this case, Lord Worth. I'm afraid you've been misinformed or hoaxed. The *Torbello* has not arrived.'

'But damn it, I've just heard – '

'One moment, please.'

The moment passed into about thirty, during which Mitchell thoughtfully brought Lord Worth a glass of scotch, which he half-consumed at one gulp. Then the voice came through again.

'Disturbing news. Not only is there no sign of your tanker, but our radar scanners show no signs of any vessel of that size being within a radius of forty miles.'

'Then what the devil can have happened to her? I was speaking to her only two or three minutes ago.'

'On her own call-sign?'

'Yes, damn it.'

'Then obviously she's come to no harm.

Lord Worth hung up without as much as a courtesy thank-you. He glowered at Larsen and Mitchell as if what had happened had been their fault. He said at length: 'I can only conclude that the captain of the *Torbello* has gone off his rocker.'

Mitchell said: 'And I conclude that he's safely under lock and key aboard his own ship.

Lord Worth was heavily ironic. 'In addition to your many other accomplishments you've now become psychic.'

'Your *Torbello* has been hijacked.'

'Hijacked! Hijacked? Now *you've* gone off your rocker. Whoever heard of a tanker being hijacked?'

'Whoever heard of a jumbo-jet being hijacked until the first one was? After what happened to the *Crusader* in Galveston the captain of the *Torbello* would have been extremely wary of being approached, far less boarded.

by any other vessel unless it were a craft with respectability beyond question. The only two such types of craft are naval or coastguard. We've heard that the Marine Gulf Corporation's survey vessel has been stolen. Many of those survey vessels are ex-coastguard with a helipad for a helicopter to carry out seismological pattern bombing The ship was called the *Hammond* With your connections ᴠou could find out in minutes.'

Lord Worth did find out in minutes. He said: 'So you're right.' He was too dumbfounded even to apologize. 'And this of course was the *Questar* that Cronkite sailed from Galveston. God only knows what name it goes under now What next, I wonder?'

Mitchell said: 'A call from Cronkite, I should think.

'What would he call me for?'

'Some outrageous demands, I should imagine. I don'ᴛ know.'

Lord Worth was nothing if not resilient. He had power-ful and influential friends. He called an admiral friend in the naval headquarters in Washington and demanded that an air-sea search unit be despatched immediately to the scene. The navy apologetically said that they would have to obtain the permission of their Commander-in-Chief – in effect, the President. The President, apparently, professed a profound if polite degree of disinterest. Neither he nor Congress had any reason to love tne oil companies who had so frequently flouted them, which was less than fair to Lord Worth who had never flouted anyone in Washington in his life. More, the search almost certainly lay outside their jurisdictional waters. Besides, it was raining in the Gulf and black as the Earl of Hell's waist-coat, and though their radar might well pick up a nundred ships in the area visual identification would be impossible

He tried the CIA Their disinterest was even more profound In the several years past they had had their fingers badly burnt in public and all their spare time was devoted to licking their wounds

The FBI curtly reminded him that their activites were purely internal and that anyway they got sea-sick whenever they ventured on water

Lord Worth considered making an appeal to the UNO, but was dissuaded by Larsen and Mitchell. Not only would the Gulf states, Venezuela, Nigeria, every Communist country and what now went by the name of the Third World – and they held the vast majority of votes in the UNO – veto any such suggestion: the UNO had no legal power to initiate any such action. Apart from that, by that time the entire UNO were probably in bed anyway

For once in his life Lord Worth appeared to be at a loss. Life, it appeared, could hold no more for him. But Lord Worth was discovering that, upon occasion, he could be as fallible as the next man: for seconds later he was at an utter and total loss

A voice-over call came through. It was, as Mitchell had predicted it would be, Cronkite. He was glad to inform Lord Worth that there was no cause for concern over the *Torbello* as she was in safe hands

'Where?' Had his daughter not been present Lord Worth would undoubtedly have qualified his question with a few choice adjectives

'I prefer not to specify exactly. Enough to say that she is securely anchored in the territorial waters of a Central American country. It is my intention to dispose of the oil to this very poor and oil-deficient country' – he did not mention that it was his intention to sell it at half-price, which would bring in a few acceptable hundred thousand dollars – 'then take the tanker out to sea and sink it in a hundred fathoms Unless, of course   '

'Unless what?' Lord Worth asked His voice had

assumed a peculiar hoarseness

'Unless you close down the Christmas tree on the *Seawitch* and immediately stop all pumping and drilling '

'Fool.'

'You said what?'

'Your thugs have already attended to that. Haven't they told you?'

'I want proof. I want Mortensen.'

Lord Worth said wearily: 'Hold on. We'll get him.'

Mitchell went to fetch him. By the time he returned, again overalled and masked, Mortensen had been thoroughly briefed. He confirmed to Cronkite that all pumping and drilling had stopped. Cronkite expressed his satisfaction and the radio link went dead. Mitchell removed the .38 from the base of Mortensen's skull and two of Palermo's men took him from the room. Mitchell took off his hood and Marina looked at him with a mixture of horror and incredulity.

She whispered: 'You were ready to kill him.'

'Not at all. I was going to pat him on the head and tell him what a good boy he was. I asked you to get off this rig '

chapter

Lord Worth had barely begun to wipe his brow when two men hurried into the room. One was Palermo and the other was one of the rig crew, Simpson, whose duty it was to monitor the sensory instruments attached to the platform's legs and the tensioning anchor cables. He was obviously in a state of considerable agitation.

Lord Worth said: 'What fresh horror does fate hold in store for us now?'

'Somebody below the rig, sir. My instruments have gone a bit haywire. Some object, something almost certainly metallic, sir, is in intermittent contact with the western leg.'

'There can be no doubt about this?' Simpson shook his head. 'Seems damnably odd that Cronkite would try to bring down the *Seawitch* with his own men on board.'

Mitchell said: 'Maybe he doesn't want to bring it down, just damage the leg enough to destroy the buoyancy in the leg and the adjacent members and to tilt the *Seawitch* so that the drill and the pumping mechanism are rendered useless. Maybe anything. Or maybe he would be prepared to sacrifice his own men to get you.' He turned to Palermo. 'I know you have scuba equipment aboard. Show me.' They left.

Marina said 'I suppose he's off to murder someone else He's not really human, is he?'

Lord Worth looked at her without enthusiasm. 'If you

call being inhuman wanting to see that you don't die, then he's inhuman. There's only one person aboard this rig he really cares for and you damned well know it. I never thought I'd be ashamed of a daughter of mine.'

Palermo had, in fact, two trained scuba divers with him, but Mitchell chose only one to accompany him. Palermo was not a man to be easily impressed but he had seen enough of Mitchell not to question his judgment. In remarkably quick time Mitchell and the other man, who went by the name of Sawyers, were dressed in scuba outfits, and were equipped with reloadable compressed air harpoon guns and sheath knives. They were lowered to the water by the only available means in such a giant TLP – in a wire-mesh cage attached to the boom of the derrick crane. Once at water level they opened the hinged door, dived and swam to the giant western leg.

Simpson had made no mistake. They were indeed at work down there, two of them, attached by airlines and cables to the shadowy outline of a vessel some twenty feet above them. Both wore powerful headlamps. They were energetically engaged in attaching limpet mines, conventional magnetic mines and wrap-round rolls of beehive amatol to the enormous leg. They had enough explosives there, Mitchell figured, to bring down the Eiffel Tower. Maybe Cronkite did intend to destroy the leg. That Cronkite was unhinged seemed more probable than not.

The two saboteurs were not only energetically engaged in their task, they were so exclusively preoccupied with it that they quite failed to notice the stealthy approach of Mitchell and Sawyers. The two scuba divers pressed their masks together, looked into each other's eyes – there was sufficient reflected light from the other divers to allow them to do this – and nodded simultaneously. Not being much given to squeamishness where potential killers were concerned, they harpooned the two saboteurs through their backs. In both cases death must have been instantaneous. Mitchell and Sawyers reloaded their compressed air harpoons then, for good measure, they sliced their two victims' breathing tubes which, as was standard, also contained the communication wires.

On the *Starlight* Easton and his crew were instantly aware that something had gone drastically wrong. The dead men were pulled up, the harpoons still embedded in their backs, and as they were being hauled over the gunwales two of the crew cried out in agony: Mitchell and Sawyers had surfaced and picked off two more targets. Whether either had been mortally or grievously injured was impossible to say, but far more than enough had happened for Easton to take off at speed, this time on his much faster diesels: the engines were admittedly noisy but the darkness was so intense that only a near-miracle would have enabled the alerted gunners on the platform to obtain an accurate fix on them.

The two scuba divers, their own headlights now switched on, swam down to the spot where the mines and explosives had been attached to the legs. There were time fuses attached to both mines and explosives. Those they detached and let fall to the bottom of the ocean. For good measure they also removed the detonators. The explosives, now harmless, they unwound and let them follow the time fuses. The mines they prudently left where they were. Both men were explosives experts but not deep water explosives experts. Mines, as many ghosts can attest to, can be very tricky and unpredictable. They consist of, as the main charge, TNT, amatol or some such conventional explosive. In their central tube they have a primer, which may consist of one of a variety of slow-burning explosives, and fitted to the top of the primer is a travelling detonator, activated by sea pressure which usually consists of seventy-seven grains of fulminate of mercury. Even with this detonator removed the primer can still detonate under immense pressure. Neither diver had any wish to blow up the pile-driven anchors or the tensioning cables attached to the anchors. Via the derrick crane they made their way back to the platform and reported to the radio room. They had to wait for some time before making their report, for Lord Worth was in a far from amicable telephone conversation with Cronkite. Marina sat apart, her hands clenched and her normally tanned face a greyish colour. She looked at Mitchell then averted her eyes as if she never wished to set eyes on him again which, at the moment, she probably didn't.

Cronkite was furious. 'You murderous bastard, Worth.' He was clearly unaware that he was talking in the presence of ladies. 'Three of my best men dead, all of them harpooned through the back.' Involuntarily, Marina looked at Mitchell again. Mitchell had the impression that he was either a monster from outer space or from the nethermost depths: at any rate, a monster.

Lord Worth was no less furious. 'It would be a pleasure to repeat the process – with you as the central figure this time.'

Cronkite choked, then said with what might have been truth: 'My intention was just temporarily to incapacitate the *Seawitch* without harming anyone aboard. But if you want to play it rough you'll have to find a new *Seawitch* in twenty-four hours. If, that is, you're fortunate enough to survive the loss of the present *Seawitch*. I'm going to blast you out of the water.'

Lord Worth was calmer now. 'It would be interesting to know how you're going to achieve that. My information is that your precious warships have been ordered back to base.'

'There's more than one way of blasting you out of the

water.' Cronkite sounded very sure of himself. 'In the meantime, I'm going to off-load the *Torbello*'s oil, then sink it.' In point of fact Cronkite had no intention of sinking the tanker: the *Torbello* was a Panamanian-registered tanker and Cronkite was not lacking in Panamanian friends: a tanker could be easily disposed of for a very considerable sum indeed. The conversation, if such an acrimonious exchange could be so called, ended abruptly.

Mitchell said: 'One thing's for sure. Cronkite is a fluent liar. He's nowhere near Central America. Not with that kind of reception. And we heard him talking to his friend Durand. He had elected not to come on this helicopter flight – which lasted only fifteen minutes. He's lurking somewhere just over the horizon.'

Lord Worth said: 'How did things go down there?'

'You heard from Cronkite. There was no trouble.'

'Do you expect more?'

'Yes. Cronkite sounds too damn confident for my liking.'

'How do you think it'll come.'

'Your guess is as good as mine. He might even try the same thing again.'

Lord Worth was incredulous. 'After what happened to him?'

'He may be relying on the unexpected. One thing I'm sure of. If he does try the same again he'll use different tactics. I'm sure he won't try an air or submarine approach, if for no other reason that he doesn't – he can't – have skilled men. So I don't think you'll require your radar or sonar watch-keepers tonight. Come to that, your radio operator may need a rest – after all, he's got an alarm call-up in his cabin. I'd keep Simpson on duty, though. Just in case our friends try for one of the legs again.'

Palermo said: 'But they'd be waiting this time. They'd

be operating close to the surface. They'd have armed guards ready and waiting to protect the divers, maybe even infra-red search-lights that we couldn't detect from the platform. You and Sawyers had luck the first time, and luck depends very much on the element of surprise: but there would be no luck this time, because there would be no surprise.'

'We don't need luck. Lord Worth wouldn't have had all those depth-charges stolen and brought aboard unless one of your men is an expert in depth-charges. You have such a man?'

'Yes.' Palermo eyed him speculatively. 'Cronin. Ex-petty officer. Why?'

'He could arrange the detonator setting so that the depth-charge would explode immediately or soon after hitting the water?'

'I should imagine so. Again, why?'

'We trundle three depth-charges along the platform to within, say, twenty-five yards of each of the legs. Your friend Cronin could advise us on this. My distance could be wrong. If Simpson detects anything on his sensors we just push one of the depth-charges over the side. The blast effect could or should have no effect on the leg concerned. I doubt if the boat with the divers would receive anything more than a severe shaking. But for divers in the water the concussive shock effects could hardly fail to be fatal.'

Palermo looked at him with cold, appraising eyes. 'For a man supposed to be on the side of the law, you, Mitchell, are the most cold-blooded bastard I've ever met.'

'If you want to die just say so. I should imagine you'd find conditions a bit uncomfortable nine hundred feet down in the Gulf. I suggest you get Cronin and a couple of your men and arrange the charges accordingly.'

Mitchell went to watch Palermo, Cronin and two of

their men at work. Cronin had agreed with Mitchell's estimate of placing the depth-charges twenty-five yards from the legs. As he stood there Marina came up to him.

She said: 'More men are going to die, aren't they, Michael?'

'I hope not.'

'But you are getting ready to kill, aren't you?'

'I'm getting ready to survive. I'm getting ready for all of us to survive.'

She took his arm 'Do you like killing?'

'No.'

'Then how come you're so good at it?'

'Somebody has to be.'

'For the good of mankind, I suppose?'

'You don't have to talk to me.' He paused and went on slowly. 'Cops kill. Soldiers kill. Airmen kill. They don't have to like it. In the First World War a fellow called Marshal Foch became the most decorated soldier of the war for being responsible for the deaths of a million men. The fact that most of them were his own men would appear to be beside the point. I don't hunt, I don't shoot game, I don't even fish. I mean, I like lamb as much as the next man but I wouldn't put a hook in its throat and drag it around a field for half an hour before it dies from agony and exhaustion. All I do is exterminate vermin. To me, all crooks, armed or not, are vermin.'

'That's why you and John got fired from the police?'

'I have to tell you that?'

'Ever killed what you, what I, would call a good person?'

'No. But unless you shut up – '

'In spite of everything, I think I might still marry you.'

'I've never asked you.'

'Well, what are you waiting for?'

Mitchell sighed, then smiled. 'Lady Marina Worth,

would you do me the honour - '

Behind them, Lord Worth coughed. Marina swung round, the expression on her face indicating that only her aristocratic upbringing was preventing her from stamping her foot. 'Daddy, you have a genius for turning up at the wrong moment.'

Lord Worth was mild. 'The right moment I would have said. My unreserved congratulations.' He looked at Mitchell. 'Well, you certainly took your time about it. Everything ship-shape and secured for the night?'

'As far as I can guess at what goes on in Cronkite's devious mind.'

'My confidence in you, my boy, is total. Well, it's bed for me - I feel, perhaps not unaccountably, extremely tired.'

Marina said: 'Me, too. Well, good night, fiancé.' She kissed him lightly and left with her father.

For once Lord Worth's confidence in Mitchell was slightly misplaced. He had made a mistake, though a completely unwitting one, in sending the radio officer off duty. For had that officer remained on duty he would undoubtedly have picked up the news flash about the theft of the nuclear weapons from the Netley Rowan Armoury: Mitchell could not have failed to put two and two together.

During the third hour of Lord Worth's conscience-untroubled sleep Mulhooney had been extremely active. He had discharged his 50,000 tons of oil and taken the *Torbello* well out to sea, far over the horizon. He returned an hour later with two companions and the ship's only motorized lifeboat with the sad news that, in the sinking of the tanker, a shattering explosion had occurred which had decimated his crew. They three were the only survivors. The 'decimated crew' were, at that moment, taking the *Torbello* south to Panama. The official condolences were widespread, apparently sincere and wholly hypocritical: when a tanker blows up its motorized lifeboat does not survive intact. The republic had no diplomatic relations with the United States and the only things they would cheerfully have extradited to that country were cholera and the bubonic plague. A private jet awaited the three at the tiny airport. Passports duly stamped, Mulhooney and his friends took out a flight plan for Guatemala

Some hours later they arrived at the Houston International Airport With much of the remaining ten million dollars still remaining at his disposal Cronkite was not the man to worry about incidental expenses. Mulhooney and his friends immediately hired a long-range helicopter and set out for the Gulf.

In the fourth hour of his sleep, which had remained undisturbed by the sound of a considerable underwater explosion, Lord Worth was unpleasantly awakened by a call from a seethingly mad Cronkite who accused him of killing two more of his men and that he, Cronkite, was going to exact a fearful vengeance. Lord Worth hung up without bothering to reply, sent for Mitchell and learned that Cronkite had indeed made another attempt to sabotage the western leg. The depth-charge had apparently done everything that had been expected of it, for their search-lights had picked up the bodies of two divers floating on the surface. The craft that had been carrying them could not have been seriously damaged, for they had heard the sound of its diesels starting up. Instead of making a straight escape, it had disappeared under the rig and by the time they had reached the other side it had so vanished into the darkness and rain that they had been unable to pick it up. Lord Worth smiled happily and went back to sleep

In the fifth hour of his sleep he would not have been smiling quite so happily if he had been aware of certain strange activities that were taking place in a remote Louisiana motel, one exclusively owned and managed by Lord Worth himself. Here it was that the *Seawitch*'s relief crews spent their weekly vacation in the strictest seclusion. In addition to abundant food, drink, films, TV and a high-class bordello that might have been run by Sally Stanford herself in her hey-day, it offered every amenity for which off-duty oil rig men could ever have wished. Not that any of them wished to step outside the compound gates: when nine out of ten men are wanted by the law, total privacy is a paramount requirement.

The intruders, some twenty in all, arrived in the middle of the night. They were led by a man – a humanoid would have been a better term for him – called Gregson: of all Cronkite's associates he was by far the most danger-ous and lethal and was possessed of the morality and instincts of a fer-de-lance with toothache. The staff were all asleep and were chloroformed before they had any opportunity of regaining consciousness.

The rig relief crew, also, were all asleep but in a some-what different fashion and for quite different reasons. Liquor is forbidden on oil rigs and the relief crews on their last night before returning to duty generally made the best of their last chance. Their dormant states ranged from the merely befuddled to the paralytic. The rounding up of them, most of whom, once afoot, remained still asleep on their feet, took no more than five minutes. The only two relatively sober members of the relief crew made to offer some show of resistance. Gregson, with a silenced Biretta, gunned them down as if they had been wild dogs

The captives were pushed inside a completely standard, albeit temporarily purloined, removal van and transported to an abandoned and very isolated warehouse on the outskirts of town. To say the least it was somewhat less than salubrious, but perfectly fitted for Gregson's purpose. The prisoners were neither bound nor gagged, which would have been pointless in the presence of two armed guards who carried the customary intimidating machine-carbines. In fact the carbines were also superfluous: the besotted captives had already drifted off into a dreamless slumber

It was in the sixth hour of Lord Worth's equally dreamless slumber that Gregson and his men lifted off in one of Lord Worth's helicopters. The two pilots had been reluctant to accept them as passengers but Schmeissers are powerful persuasive agents.

It was in the seventh hour of Lord Worth's slumber that Mulhooney and his two colleagues touched down on the empty helipad of the *Georgia*. As Cronkite's own helicopter was temporarily marooned on the *Seawitch* he had no compunction in impounding both the helicopter and its hapless pilot.

At almost exactly the same moment another helicopter touched down on the *Seawitch* and a solitary passenger and pilot emerged. The passenger was Dr Greenshaw, and he looked, and was, a very tired, elderly man. He went straight to the sick-bay and, without as much as trying to remove his clothes, lay down on one of the cots and composed himself for sleep. He should, he supposed, have reported to Lord Worth that his daughter Melinda and John Roomer were in good hands and in good shape: but good news could wait

*

204

On the eighth hour, with the dawn in the sky, Lord Worth, a man who enjoyed his sleep, awoke, stretched himself luxuriously, pulled on his splendidly embroidered dressing-gown and strolled out on to the platform. The rain had stopped, the sun was tipping the horizon and there was every promise of a beautiful day to come. Privately congratulating himself on his prescience that no trouble would occur during the night, he retired to his quarters to perform his customary and leisurely morning ablutions.

Lord Worth's self-congratulation on his prescience were entirely premature. Fifteen minutes earlier the radio operator, newly returned to duty, had picked up a news broadcast that he didn't like at all and gone straight to Mitchell's room. Like every man on board, even including Larsen and Palermo, he knew that the man to contact in an emergency was Mitchell: the thought of alerting Lord Worth never entered his head.

He found Mitchell shaving. Mitchell looked tired, less than surprising as he had spent most of the night awake. Mitchell said: 'No more trouble, I hope?'

'I don't know.' He handed Mitchell a strip of teletype. It read: 'Two tactical nuclear weapons stolen from the Netley Rowan Armoury yesterday afternoon. Intelligence suspects they are being flown or helicoptered south over Gulf of Mexico to an unknown destination. A world-wide alert has been issued. Anyone able to provide information should – '

'Jesus! Get hold of this armoury any way you can. Use Lord Worth's name. With you in a minute '

Mitchell was with him in half a minute. The operator said: 'I'm through already. Not much co-operation, though.'

'Give me that phone. Hello? My name's Mitchell. Who's speaking, please?'

'Colonel Pryce.' The tone wasn't exactly distant, just a senior officer talking to a civilian.

'I work for Lord Worth. You can check that with the Lauderdale Police, the Pentagon or the Secretary of State.' He said to the operator, but loudly enough that Pryce could hear: 'Get Lord Worth here. I don't care if he is in his bloody bath, just get him here now. Colonel Pryce, an officer of your standing should know that Lord Worth's daughters have been kidnapped. I have been engaged to recover them and this I have done. More importantly, this oil rig, the *Seawitch*, is under threat of destruction. Two attempts have already been made. They were unsuccessful. Further questioning of the Pentagon will confirm that they have stopped three foreign warships headed here for the purpose of destroying the *Seawitch*. I believe those nuclear weapons are heading this way. I want information about those tactical weapons and I must warn you that Lord Worth will interpret any failure to provide this information as a gross dereliction of duty. And you know the immense power Lord Worth has.'

There was a far from subtle change in Colonel Pryce's tone. 'It's quite unnecessary to threaten me.'

'One moment. Lord Worth's just arrived.' Mitchell gave a brief résumé of what he had said, making sure that Pryce could hear every word that was spoken.

'Nuclear bloody bombs! That's why Cronkite said he could blast us out of the water!' Lord Worth snatched the phone from Mitchell. 'Lord Worth here. I have a hot line to the Secretary of State, Dr Belton. I could catch him in fifteen seconds. Want I should do that?'

'That will not be necessary, Lord Worth.'

'Then give us a detailed description of those damned evil things and tell us how they work.'

Pryce, almost eagerly, gave the description. It was

almost precisely similar to the one that Captain Martin had given to the bogus Colonel Farquharson 'But Martin was a new officer and shaky on his details. The nuclear devices – you can hardly call them bombs – are probably twice as effective as he said. They took the wrong type – those devices have no black button to shut off in an emergency. And they have a ninety-minute setting, not sixty. *And* they can be radio activated.'

'Something complicated? I mean, a VHF number or something of the kind?'

'Something very uncomplicated. You can't expect a soldier in the heat of battle to remember abstruse numbers. It's simply a pear-shaped device with a plastic seal. Strip that off and turn a black switch through three-hundred and sixty degrees. It is important to remember that turning this switch off will de-activate the detonating mechanism in the nuclear device. It can be turned on again at any time.'

'If it should be used against us? We have a huge oil storage tank nearby. Wouldn't this cause a massive oil slick?'

'My dear fellow, oil is by nature combustible and much more easily vaporized than steel.'

'Thank you.'

'Seems to be you want a squadron of supersonic fighter-bombers out there. But I'll have to get Pentagon permission first.'

'Thank you again.'

Lord Worth and Mitchell left for the former's quarters. Lord Worth said: 'Two things. We're only assuming, although it would be dangerous not to assume, that those damned things are meant for us. Besides, if we keep our radar, sonar and sensory posts manned I don't see how Cronkite could approach and deliver those damned things.'

'It's difficult to see how. But then it's difficult to figure out that devious devil's cast of mind.'

From Lord Worth's helicopter Gregson made contact with the *Georgia*. 'We're fifteen miles out.'

Cronkite himself replied. 'We'll be airborne in ten.'

A wall radio crackled in Lord Worth's room. 'Helicopter approaching from the north-east.'

'No worry. Relief crew.'

Lord Worth had gone back to his shower when the relief helicopter touched down. Mitchell was in his laboratory, looking very professional in his white coat and glasses. Dr Greenshaw was still asleep.

Apart from gagging and manacling the pilots, the helicopter passengers offered them no violence. They disembarked in quiet and orderly fashion. The drill duty crew observed their arrival without any particular interest. They had been well trained to mind their own business and had highly personal reasons for not fraternizing with unknowns. And the new arrivals were unknowns. Off the coast Lord Worth owned no fewer than nine oil rigs – all legally leased and paid for – and, for reasons best known to his devious self, was in the habit of regularly rotating his drill crews. The new arrivals carried the standard shoulder-slung clothes-bags. Those bags did indeed contain a minimal amount of clothes, but not clothing designed to be worn: the clothes were there merely to conceal and muffle the shape of the machine-pistols and other more deadly weapons inside the bags.

Thanks to the instructions he had received from Cronkite via Durand, Gregson knew exactly where to go. He noted the presence of two idly patrolling guards and marked them down for death.

He led his men to the Oriental quarters where they placed their bags on the platform and unzipped them. Windows were smashed and what followed was sheer savage massacre. Within half a dozen seconds of machine-gun fire, bazooka fire and incinerating flame-throwers, all of which had been preceded by a flurry of tear-gas bombs, all screaming inside had ceased. The two advancing guards were mown down even as they drew their guns. The only survivor was Larsen, who had been in his own private room in the back: Palermo and all his men were dead.

Four people appeared almost at the same instant from the quarters at the end of the block. Soundproofed though those quarters were, the noise outside had been too penetrating not to be heard. There were four of them, two men in white coats, a man in a Japanese kimono and a black-haired guard in a wrap. One of Gregson's men fired twice at the nearest white-coated figure and Mitchell staggered and fell backwards to the deck. Gregson brutally smashed the wrist of the man who had fired, who screamed in agony as the gun fell from his shattered hand.

'You bastard idiot!' Gregson's voice was as vicious as his appearance. 'The hard men only, Mr Cronkite said.'

Gregson was nothing if not organized. He detailed five groups of two men. One group herded the drilling rig crew into the Occidental quarters. The second, third and fourth went respectively to the sensory room, the sonar room and the radar room. There they tied up but did not otherwise harm the operators, before they riddled all the equipment with a burst of machine-gun bullets. For all practical purposes the *Seawitch* was now blind, deaf and benumbed. The fifth group went to the radio room, where the operator was tied up but his equipment left intact.

Dr Greenshaw approached Gregson. 'You are the leader?'

'Yes.'

'I'm a doctor.' He nodded to Mitchell, whose white coat accentuated his blood and who was rolling about in a convincing manner, Marina bending over him with bitter tears rolling down her cheeks. 'He's hurt bad. Can I take him into the sick-bay and patch him up?'

'We have no quarrel with you,' Gregson said, which was, unwittingly, the most foolish remark he'd ever made in his life.

Dr Greenshaw helped the weak and staggering Mitchell into the sick-bay where, the door closed behind him, he made an immediate and remarkable recovery. Marina stared at him in astonishment, then in something approaching anger.

'Why you deceiving, double-crossing – '

'That's no way to talk to a sick man.' He was pulling off his white coat, jacket and shirt. 'Never seen you cry before. Makes you look even more beautiful. And that's real blood.' He turned to Dr Greenshaw. 'Superficial wound on the left shoulder, a scratch on the right forearm. Dead-eyed Dick himself. Now make a real good job on me, Doc. Right forearm bandaged from elbow to wrist. Left arm bandaged from shoulder to above the elbow with a lovely big sling. Marina, even ravishing beauties like you carry talcum powder. I hope you're no exception.'

Not yet mollified, she said stiffly: 'I have some. Baby powder,' she added nastily.

'Get it, please.'

Five minutes later Mitchell had been rendered into the epitome of the walking wounded. His right arm was heavily bandaged and his left arm was swathed in white from shoulder to wrist. The sling was nothing short of voluminous. His face was very pale indeed. He left for his

210

room and returned a few seconds later.

'Where have you been?' Marina asked suspiciously.

He reached inside the depths of the sling and pulled out his silenced .38. 'Fully loaded.' He returned it to its hiding place where it was quite invisible.

'Never give up, do you?' Her voice held a curious mixture of awe and bitterness.

'Not when I'm about to be vaporized.'

Dr Greenshaw stared at him. 'What in God's name do you mean?'

'Our good friend Cronkite has pinched a couple of tactical nuclear weapons. He intends to finish off the *Seawitch* in a style of befitting splendour. He should be here about now. Now, Doc, I would like you to do something for me. Take the biggest medical bag you have and tell Gregson that it is your humanitarian duty to go inside that shambles that used to be the Occidental quarters to succour any that may be dying or, if necessary, to put them out of their agony. They have, I know, a respectable supply of hand-grenades in there. I'd like some.'

'No sooner said than done. God, you look awful. Destroys my faith in myself as a doctor.'

They went outside. Cronkite's helicopter was indeed just touching down. Cronkite himself was the first out, followed by Mulhooney, the three bogus officers who had stolen the nuclear weapons, the commandeered pilot and lastly Easton. Easton was the unknown quantity. Mitchell did not appreciate it at the time but Easton's *Starlight* had been so badly damaged by the depth-charge that it was no longer serviceable. Less than four miles away what appeared to be a coastguard cutter was heading straight for the *Seawitch*. It required no guessing to realize that this was the missing *Hammond*, the infamous *Questar*, the present *Georgia*.

Dr Greenshaw approached Gregson. 'Mind if I have a

look at the little you've left of those quarters? Maybe there's someone still alive in there: more likely there's someone who requires a little kindly euthanasia.'

Gregson pointed to an iron door. 'I'm more interested in who's in there. Spicer' – this to one of his men – 'a bazooka shot at that lock.'

'That's hardly necessary,' Greenshaw said mildly. 'A knock from me is all that is required. That's Commander Larsen, the boss of the oil rig. He's no enemy of yours. He just sleeps here because he likes his privacy.' Dr Greenshaw knocked. 'Commander Larsen. It's okay. It's me, Greenshaw. Come on out. If you don't there are some people who are going to blast your door down and you with it. Come on, man. I'm not saying this under duress.'

There was the turning of a heavy key and Larsen emerged. He looked dazed, almost shell-shocked, as well he might. He said: 'What the hell goes on?'

'You've been taken over, friend,' Gregson said. Larsen was dressed, Greenshaw was pleased to note, in a voluminous lumber-jacket, zipped around the waist 'Search him.' They searched and found nothing

'Where's Scoffield?' Larsen said.

Greenshaw said: 'In the other quarters. He should be okay.'

'Palermo?'

'Dead. And all his men. At least I think so. I'm just going to have a look-see.' Stooping his shoulders to look more nearly eighty than his seventy years, Dr Greenshaw shambled along the shattered corridor, but he could have saved himself the trouble of acting. Gregson had just met Cronkite outside the doorway and the two men were talking in animated and clearly self-congratulatory terms.

After the first few steps Greenshaw realized that there could be nobody left alive in that charnel-house. Those who were dead were very dead indeed, most of them destroyed beyond recognition, either by machine-gun fire, shattered by bazookas or shrivelled by the flame-throwers. But he did find the primary reason for his visit there – a box of hand-grenades in prime condition and a couple of Schmeisser sub-automatics, fully loaded. A few of the grenades he stuffed into the bottom of his medical bag. He peered out of one of the shattered windows at the back and found the area below in deep shadow. He carefully lowered some grenades to the platform and laid the two Schmeissers beside them. Then he made his way outside again.

It was apparent that Cronkite and Lord Worth had already met, although the meeting could not have been a normal one. Lord Worth was lying apparently senseless on his back, blood flowing from smashed lips and apparently broken nose, while both cheeks were badly bruised. Marina was bending over him, dabbing at his wounds with a flimsy handkerchief. Cronkite, his face unmarked but his knuckles bleeding, had apparently, for the moment at least, lost interest in Lord Worth, no doubt waiting until Lord Worth had regained full consciousness before starting in on him again.

Lord Worth whispered between smashed lips: 'Sorry, my darling, sorry, my beloved. My fault and all my fault The end of the road.'

'Yes.' Her voice was as low as his own, but strangely there were no tears in her eyes. 'But not for us. Not while Michael is alive.'

Lord Worth looked at Michael through rapidly closing eyes. 'What can a cripple like that do?'

She said with low but utter conviction: 'He'll kill Cronkite and all his evil friends.'

He tried to smile but his smashed lips wouldn't let him. 'I thought you hated killing.'

'Not vermin Not people who do things like this to my dad '

Mitchell spoke quietly to Dr Greenshaw, then both men approached Cronkite and Gregson, who broke off what appeared to be either a discussion or an argument. Dr Greenshaw said: 'I'm afraid you've done your damn murderous work all too well, Gregson. There's not a soul in there even recognizable as a human being.'

Cronkite said: 'Who's he?'

'A doctor.'

Cronkite looked at Mitchell, who was looking worse by the minute. 'And this?'

'A scientist. Shot by mistake.'

'He's in great pain,' Greenshaw said. 'I've no X-ray equipment but I suspect the arm's broken just below the shoulder '

Cronkite was almost jovial, the joviality of a man now almost detached from reality. 'An hour from now he won't be feeling a thing.'

Greenshaw said wearily: 'I don't know what you mean. I just want to take him to the sick-bay and give him a pain-killing injection.'

'Certainly. I'd like everyone to be fully prepared for what's about to happen to him.'

'And what's that?'

'Later, later.'

Greenshaw and the unsteady Mitchell moved off. They reached the sick-bay, passed inside, went through the opposite side and made their unobserved way to the radio room. Greenshaw stood guard just inside the door while Mitchell, ignoring the bound operator, went straight to the transceiver. He raised the *Roamer* inside twenty seconds.

'Captain Conde, please.'

'Speaking.'

'Next circuit out to the oil tank get round behind it then head south at full speed. The *Seawitch* has been taken over but I'm certain there's nobody here who can operate the anti-aircraft guns. Stop at twenty miles and issue a general warning to all ships and aircraft not to approach within twenty miles of the *Seawitch*. You have its co-ordinates?'

'Yes. But why – '

'Because there's going to be a mighty big bang. Christ's sake, don't argue.'

'Don't argue about what?' a voice behind Mitchell said.

Mitchell turned round slowly. The man behind the pistol was smiling a smile that somehow lacked a genuine warmth. Greenshaw had been pushed to one side and the gun moved in a slow arc covering them both. 'I've a feeling that Gregson would like to see you both.'

Mitchell rose, turned, half-staggered and clutched his left forearm inside the sling. Greenshaw said sharply: 'God's sake, man, can't you see he's ill?'

The man glanced at Greenshaw for a second but a second was all that Mitchell would ever require. The bullet from the silenced .38 took him through the heart. Mitchell peered through the doorway. There was a fair degree of shadow there, no one in sight and the edge of the platform not more than twenty feet away. A few seconds later the dead man vanished over the edge. Mitchell and Greenshaw returned to the main body of the company via the sick-bay. Cronkite and Gregson were still in deep discussion. Larsen stood some distance apart, apparently in a state of profound dejection. Greenshaw approached him and said quietly: 'How do you feel?'

'How would you feel if you knew they intended to kill us all?'

'You'll feel better by and by. Round the back of the building, when you get the chance, you'll find some hand-grenades which should rest comfortably inside that lumber-jacket of yours. You'll also find two loaded Schmeissers. I have a few grenades in my medical bag here. And Mitchell has his silenced .38 inside his sling.'

Larsen took care not to show his feelings. He looked as morose as ever. All he said was: 'Boy, oh boy, oh boy.'

Lord Worth was on his feet now, supported by his daughter. Mitchell joined them. 'How do you feel, sir?'

Lord Worth spoke or rather mouthed his words with understandable bitterness. 'I'm in great shape'

'You'll feel better soon.' He lowered his voice and spoke to Marina. 'When I give the word, say you want to go to the ladies' room. But don't go there. Go to the generator room. You'll see a red lever there marked "Deck Lights". Pull it down. After you count twenty put it on again.'

Cronkite and Gregson appeared to have finished their discussion. From Cronkite's smile it appeared that his view had prevailed. Lord Worth, Marina, Larsen, Green-shaw and Mitchell stood together, a forlorn and huddled group. Facing them were the serried ranks of Cronkite, Mulhooney, Easton, the bogus Colonel Farquharson, Lieutenant-Colonel Dewings, Major Breckley, Gregson and all his killers, a most formidable group and armed to the teeth.

Cronkite spoke to a man by his side. 'Check.'

The man lifted a walkie-talkie, spoke into it and nodded. He said to Cronkite: 'Charges secured in position.'

'Excellent. Tell them to steam due north for twenty miles and remain there.' This was done. Unfortunately for Cronkite, his view to the west was blocked by the shattered building behind him and he could not see that the *Roamer* was already steaming steadily to the south.

Even had he had a clear view it would hardly have mattered: Conde had prudently extinguished every light aboard the *Roamer*.

Cronkite smiled. 'Well, Lord Worth, it's the end of the road for both you and the *Seawitch*. Even a billionaire can step out of his class. I have two nuclear devices attached to the western leg of the *Seawitch*.' He dug into a pocket and produced a black pear-shaped metal container. 'The radio-active detonating device. You will not fail to observe this small switch here. It's supposed to be good for ninety minutes, but I have already run off forty minutes of it. Fifty more minutes and poof! the *Seawitch*, you, Lord Worth, and everyone aboard will be vaporized. Nobody will feel a thing, I assure you.'

'You mean you intend to kill all my innocent employees aboard the rig? Your mind, Cronkite, has totally gone You are stark raving mad.'

'Never saner. Can't have any witnesses left who can identify us. Then we destroy two of the helicopters, immobilize your derrick crane, smash your radio room and take off in the other two helicopters. You may, of course, contemplate jumping into the Gulf, but your chances of survival would be about the same as a suicide jumping off the Golden Gate bridge.'

Mitchell nudged Marina. She said in a faint voice. 'May I go to the ladies' room?'

Cronkite was joviality itself. 'Certainly. But be quick about it.'

Fifteen seconds later the deck lights went out.

It was Mitchell, with his unique capacity to see in the dark, who ran round the corner of the shattered building, retrieved the two Schmeissers – he didn't bother about the grenades – returned and thrust one into Larsen's hands. Twelve seconds had elapsed but in eight seconds two men with sub-machine-guns can achieve an extra-

ordinary amount of carnage Larsen was firing blind but
Mitchell could see and pick out his targets. They were
helped, in a most haphazard fashion, by Dr Greenshaw
who flung grenades at random inflicting even more
damage on the already shattered building but not
actually injuring anyone.

The lights came on again.

There were still seven people left alive – Cronkite,
Mulhooney, Easton, Gregson and three of his men. To
those seven Mitchell said: 'Lay down your arms.' Shattered and stunned though the survivors were, they still
had enough of their wits to comply at once.

Marina arrived back and was promptly sick in a very
unladylike fashion.

Mitchell put down his Schmeisser and advanced on
Cronkite. 'Give me that detonating device.'

Cronkite removed it slowly from his pocket, suddenly
turned the switch and lifted his arm preparatory to
throwing it over the side. Whatever else, it would have
meant the destruction of the *Seawitch*. Cronkite screamed
in agony as the bullet from the silenced .38 shattered his
right elbow. Mitchell caught the detonating device even
before it could reach the deck.

He said to Larsen: 'Are there two absolutely secure
places with no windows and iron doors which can be
securely locked without any possibility of opening them
from the inside?'

'Just two. Safe as the Fort Knox vaults. Along here.'

'Search them and search them thoroughly Make sure
they haven't even a penknife.'

Larsen searched. 'Not even a penknife.' He led them to
a steel-reinforced cell-like structure, and he and Mitchell
ushered them inside.

In spite of his agony Cronkite said: 'You're not going
to leave us in here, for God's sake!'

'Just as you were going to leave us' Mitchell paused then added soothingly: 'As you said, you won't feel a thing.' He closed the door, double-locked it and put the key in his pocket. He said to Larsen: 'The other cell?'

'Along here.'

'This is madness!' Lord Worth's voice was almost a shout. 'The *Seawitch* is safe now. Why in God's name destroy it?'

Mitchell ignored him. He glanced at the timing device on the detonator. 'Twenty-nine minutes to go. We'd better move.' He placed the device on the floor of the cell, locked the door and sent the key spinning far out over the Gulf. 'Get the men out of the Occidental buildings, free the men in the sensory, radar, sonar and radio rooms and make sure that all the helicopter pilots are safe.' He glanced at his watch. 'Twenty-five minutes.'

Everyone moved with astounding alacrity except for Lord Worth, who just stood around with a stunned look on his face. Larsen said: 'Is there a need for all this mad rush?'

Mitchell said mildly: 'How do we know that the settings on that detonator are accurate?'

The mad rush redoubled itself. Thirteen minutes before the deadline the last of the helicopters took off and headed south. The first to land on the *Roamer*'s helipad held Mitchell, Larsen, Lord Worth and his daughter, in addition to the doctor and several rig men, while the other helicopters still hovered overhead. They were still only about fourteen miles south of the *Seawitch*, which was as far as the *Roamer* had succeeded in getting in that time, but Mitchell reckoned the margin of safety more than sufficient. He spoke to Conde who assured him that every vessel and aircraft had been warned to keep as far away as possible from the danger area

When the *Seawitch* blew up, dead on schedule, it did so

with a spectacular effect that would have satisfied even the most ghoulish. There was even a miniature mushroom cloud such as the public had become accustomed to in the photographs of detonating regular megaton atom bombs. Seventeen seconds later those in the *Roamer* heard the thunderclap of sound and shortly afterwards a series of miniature but harmless tidal waves rocked, but did not unduly disturb, the *Roamer*. After Mitchell had told Conde to broadcast the news to all aircraft and shipping he turned to find a stony-faced Marina confronting him.

'Well, you've lost Daddy his *Seawitch*. I do hope you're satisfied with yourself.'

'My, my, how bitter we are. Yes, quite a satisfactory job, even if I have to sav it myself, for obviously no one else is going to.'

'Why? Why? Why?'

'Every man who died there was a murderer, some mass murderers. They might have escaped to countries with no extradition treaties with the States. Even if caught their cases might have dragged on for years. Proof would have been very difficult to obtain. And, of course, parole after a few years. This way, we know they'll never kill again.'

'And it was worth it to lose Daddy's pride and joy?'

'Listen, stupid. My father-in-law-to-be is – '

'That he'll never be '

'So okay. That old geezer is almost as big a crook as any of them. He associated with and hired for lethal purposes known and convicted criminals. He broke into two federal armouries and mounted the equipment on the *Seawitch*. Had the *Seawitch* survived, federal investigators would have been aboard within the hour. He'd have got at least fifteen to twenty years in prison, and he'd probably have died in prison.' Her eyes were wide, partly with fear, partly with understanding. 'But now every last tiny shred of evidence lies vaporized at the bottom of the Gulf of

Mexico A little in radiation clouds, maybe, but that's not the point. Nothing can ever be traced against him.'

'That's really why you vaporized the *Seawitch*?'

'Why should I admit anything to an ex-fiancée?'

'Mrs Michael Mitchell,' she mused. 'I suppose I could go through life with a worse name.'